Be at a loss

Exodus
By
Summer Storm

Hey y'all. My name is Killa. At least that's

what they call me. I don't believe that that's what my

mama named me but that's all I knowed ever since I

can remember. I heared it said that out of the

fourteen kids my mama birthed I was the biggest one

weighing somewheres in the name of thirteen pounds.

Said my birth was a real killa and that was how I

come to get my name. Like I said that's the only

name I've ever known although I ain't exactly sho

how I come to get it or who attached it to me.

Me. Well I don't exactly see myself as no

killa but being that I was the biggest, most largest on

the McCLowry plantation I was just naturally assigned to butcher the hogs, cows and any other large livestock around the place. I guess this cemented my name and after a while it just became second-nature to me. Guess it's like the old folks say—you know—a self fulfillin' prophecy and bein' that's not how I wants to be seen I fights it. Sometimes though, it becomes quite necessary in these days of bondage. You can't just call yo'self a man and allow yourself to be treated like a boy. Early on I established the fact that dying just didn't mean that much to me and I would easily die before I let you disrespect me and treat me like less than a man.

When I was younger, in my late teens I had a few scrapes with massa's overseer, some ol' poor white trash Massa McClowry dredged up on one of his drinkin' binges down Natchez way. Sayed, he liked the man's thinkin' when it come to his handlin' of chattel or niggas as we is more commonly referred to. You take the the 'd' offa devil and that's what he was. Pure ol' uncut, unadulterated, evil. Iffen he wasn't checkin' out the petticoats on some twelve-year-old child, he goin' after they mother, or whippin' a nigga's head outta outright meanness. You didn't have to do nothin' and he'd ride up next to you and haul off and just swat you for no reason.

Rode up beside me one day and just sat there on that big, brown, sorrel of his. I'm lean't over croppin' tobaccy and I know he's got a notion to test me. And I stands up and looks this cracker squarely in the eye. Now that in itself was enough to get a nigga tarred and feathered but like I said I's a man and will be respected just like any other man. Anyways, I stands there—all six nine of me—and like I said he sitting high atop his horse and I's still looking at him eye-to-eye and I's thinkin'. White man is you ready to meet your maker cause if you even think you gonna hit me with any parts of that there whip I' afraid I'm going to have to introduce

you to the good Lord. I guess he knew he'd met his

Waterloo when he run up against me. But what I

have found all too often is that white folk will try you

knowing full well that they are going on a lose-lose

expedition and yet they will still try.

A few weeks later, he came up to me again

quite brazenly and made the comment that as big as I

was I should be able to do twice the work of anyone

out there and there were women croppin' more

tobaccy than me. I heard him but pretended he

wasn't there which annoyed him greatly. He drew

back on that whip and let it fly but instead of

cowering away from it I grabbed it yanking him down

from his horse causing a great commotion. There was

a cheer that went up from among my counter parts,

but I was oblivious to all but this cracker who now

lay at my feet.

I could have very well snapped his throat but there were far too many witnesses and though most would be tight-lipped about anything that happened to that cracker. But I knew that there was always the one who would sell you out for an extra biscuit at dinner. Still, I let him know in no uncertain terms that if he ever drew his hand back to strike me he would be drawing back a nub the next time. It was not long afterwards when there was no word from the ova' seer. He just vanished into thin air. Much of the talk around this time was that he left out of sheer embarrassment. To have a slave embarrass you was the worst thing that could ever happen to a white man. There were only a few incidents of this happening without severe repercussions. This was one of them. There was other talk that I had disposed of the man. It was all just talk if you ask me, but Massa McClowry was in no rush to hire another ova' seer.

Most days are the same. We niggas that works the fields gets up with the chickens and works til' we can't see no more at night. The days be long and you gots to put your mind somewheres else and just pray yo' body can endure. It ain't bad as you think now abouts. We know what kind of harvest the massa be lookin for, so we just goes about our work like we working for our own benefit. We take pride in our work even though it don't belong to us and we don't prosper from its sale. But with no ova'seer I believe one of the reasons we work so hard and take such pride in our work is because we all da time trying to prove to massa that we human too and don't need no ova' seer standing over us with a whip. Just tell us what you need done and we'll get it done. We work in groups. It's me, my sister Elise, Phoenix and Young Buck. We all in our twenties I suppose—well close as I can gather—anyway we all come up together. We seen our family members sold off and we are all that remains. We cried at the time and we promised ourselves that we would never let that happen to us. We took a bond to die before we were split apart. And we remained loyal to that. There were other things we agreed to as well, but we can discuss those at a later time.

In any case, these are my family now. I mean that. We look out for each other and we handle our business when things need to be handled. Been doing it for years now and I think people have come to respect us. No one messes with any of us and that goes for white folks and Coloreds. There's a sort of mystery surrounding us, and I can only imagine the kind of lore that comes from those forever yarning stories about us.

"But anyway, that's enough about me. Come on fella, I want you to meet me my folks. I think you gonna like 'em. They good people."

"Elise, Phoenix, Buck this here's Moses. Believe it or not this here niggra Moses ain't tryna escape and run North. This here niggra is a free man that come from Boston down South. When every nigga in Dixie is tryna get North he comes south," Killa commented shaking his head.

"Where you find this fool at?" Elise said grinning widely.

Moses smiled broadly as well. Alas, she was the prettiest thing he'd ever had the opportunity to come across.

"Lord! Will you look at that smile? My goodness I think our new friend Moses has been snake bit," Phoenix said grinning broadly. "Looks like Elise has caught another one in her web."

"I thought the way the story went was that Moses led his people out of inequity? I didn't know he actually would fall victim to the inequities." Buck teased.

"All a you need to hush. If that man likes what he sees, then who are you to try and blind him. But seriously suh, is you addle brained in the head or what? I do believe that iffen you ask any niggra below the Mason Dixie Line what their dream was they would to a man say, to go North to freedom and here you is coming to all this pain and hardship. Please explain why before I commit to making you my husband. I need to know you are of sound mind and body."

Moses found a seat on an old hollow log across from the young woman. She had to be of some royal family in the old country he thought to himself. She had to be destined to become someone's queen when her life like so many others had been interrupted by the slave catchers intent on turning a profit. This one they referred to as Elise must have brought a pretty penny at the auction block and yet how her plight had swung like the mighty pendulum

"No problem. I guess you all know by now that President Lincoln was assassinated?"

Phoenix, Killa and Buck all shook their heads no.

There's a new president now. Don't know iffen ya heard of him. His name is Johnson. Andrew Johnson. And he's no Lincoln that's for sure. He's a Democrat from Tennessee. Lincoln made him his vice president to get these Southern Crackers to vote for him but not in a million years would anybody have ever expected for him to become president. And he's in there trying to take care of these southern crackers. He done repealed or rolled back a lot of Mr. Lincoln's plans for us niggras. Ain't no more forty acres and a mule. Nah, we niggras just be out here floundering now that the slavery is officially over with no idea where to go or what to do. And in more situations than not are just like you."

"And how do we appear to be to you Mr,
Moses?"

"With all due respect to you three it appears
that many of the niggras I come across when slavery
ended had no plan as to what a niggra was supposed
to do to support hisself. And so, with no plan or idea
of how he was supposed to feed hisself and his family
he come right back to the only thing he'd ever known.
Pickin' cotton and croppin' tobacco for massa."

"Is that how you see us?"

"No. It is true that you four are resigned here
for some reason but iffen I was to guess it's only 'til
you have solidified your plans, whatever they might
be. You four are waiting for something of that much
I know. You may even be ready to make that journey
on my return. I see the longing in each of your eyes.

Ya know, to be honest, I am surprised more of
us didn't go for Mr. Lincoln's Homestead Act. He

was basically giving away land out west. All a niggra had to do was go claim it and settle it."

"But then a niggra say, 'Hell I know what kind of devil I gots to deal with here. That whole western thing come with a whole new host of unknown demons. At least I know what I gots to deal with here. The devil familiar here," Killa commented.

"That's true. I hate to refer to you to you by that name. I know I just met you, but I see so much more. Do you have a last name?"

"Same as everyone else's on the place. McClowry. I don't believe I had a choice in that one either."

"Well, Mr. McClowry I do suppose you're right. It is fear of the unknown and the way we have been brainwashed to believe that we cannot make it without massa."

"The way you talk it's a wonder that you haven't been hung up a long time ago free man or no free man."

"I am with family and so I feel free to be myself and not hide anything. But trust I didn't get to be my age by being no fool. I know how to tone it down when need be. I guess a niggra in these days and times can't never forget to drop his eyes and check hisself."

"Oh, he can forget alright and find hisself hanging from a tree somewheres," Buck added. "But let's get back to Lincoln's replacement. What else has he done in regard to niggras and the Reconstruction effort?"

"As I said he's a southerner at heart and now that he has the opportunity he's doing his best to appease these crackers in every way he can and it's to hell wit' you niggras. You know business as usual. Massa's back in the White House. He removed the federal troops that Lincoln left in place to insure our safety. And not only did he remove them he allowed the southern slaves to enlist the Black Codes."

"And what pray tell are the Black Codes?" Phoenix inquired.

"Come on Moses. Are you ready? Miss Maya is known for going to bed at the crack of dusk and it's damn there that now. Sorry it took me so long."

"I want to know about these so-called Black Codes when you return."

"I will not forget Phoenix," the two men said standing and shaking hands. "I believe it is important to know everything there is to know in order for us to move forward as people."

"No one is more informed than you Phoenix. When's the last time massa had a chance to read his own newspaper?" Buck said laughing.

"Better yet does Mr. McClowry even know that he subscribes to the newspaper?" Killa said doubling over laughing.

"We'll talk," Moses said rushing to catch up with Elise who was now walking at quite a brisk pace that left Moses gasping for breath.

"It's right over this next rise," Elise said pointing to a rather steep hill which looked like Mt. Kilimanjaro to Moses who had to admit to being a bit out of shape. He wanted nothing more than the opportunity to speak to Elise in private and now that the time had presented itself he found himself unable to. Finally, able to grasp his breath and regain his composure he found himself outside Miss Maya's quarters.

"Who dat?"

"It's me Miss Maya," Elise said.

"Oh, hey child. I ain't seen you in a minute gal. I was hoping that you didn't take anything said the last time we spoke as something friendship ending. Was just voicing my opinion is all. You know me," the tall, buxom woman said. Standing a shade over six feet. Moses had met her kind before. She was a free Black woman in bondage. That was the case, but it had come to be known that Miss Maya commanded respect because she was not afraid and aside from Killa was the only colored person that had their way around the place.

Miss Maya gained the respect of both Colored and white because she was never one to hide from the truth and would speak it clearly to anyone who asked. I suppose that's why everyone on this here place respects and relies on her for keeping the order since massa ain't never here and missy is darn near useless. She's the one that runs this here place and the reason it's so successful. Beautiful woman too and knows how to use every asset she's got in procuring what it is she wants or perceives we needs. Massa is damn near at her disposal. He just plain weak for her and in his mind and mine this is the woman he should have married in a perfect world.

"No, ma'am. How could I get angry for you just being honest?"

"Glad you feel that way. I'd hate for us to let anything come between us. Our people need to see us as a united front in this war against our own injustice."

"You are so right my sista," the two women said embracing each other and Moses noticed that both women were crying quietly. There was oh so much pain in this land of the free and home of the brave.

"So, what brings you here today and who is this handsome gentleman that you've failed to introduce me to."

Elise couldn't help but grin.

"I'm sorry Maya this is Moses and the reason we are here today. Moses has been North and is a free man with papers, but he's traveled back seven times to search for his mother and to help others escape North."

"That is commendable Moses. You said you were trying to locate your mother?"

"Yes ma'am. She was a cook for the Johansen's up in the Adam's Farm area."

"Gertrude?"

"Yes," Moses shouted. "That's my mother's name. Did you know her?"

"Yes. Gertrude and I were good friends and attended the same church. It wasn't until a week after she'd been sold that I was even informed of it. In fact the driver from the Johansen's came down to deliver massa a letter when I asked him to take her some pie I'd entered in the county fair and he informed me that my friend Gertrude had been sold."

"Did he tell you where?" Moses was pleading now.

"No. He couldn't but I knew Gertrude and I knew if anyone would get in touch it would be her and a couple of weeks later she did. Hold on just a second," the tall woman said standing now and letting the long flowing gown swirl around her thick, caramel thighs before throwing a seductive glance in Moses' direction.

"So, you're my Gerty's oldest. Am I correct? The one she was so proud of for taking his chances and gong North to finish his education?"

"Ye ma'am that would be me," Moses said watching the woman closely as she reentered the room a stack of letters in her hands.

"These are from your mother," the tall woman said handing Moses the letters before having a seat across from him and scribbling on a piece of paper.

"Here's the address," Maya said handing Moses the piece of paper.

"Oh my God. Miss Maya. You've been a godsend. I've been trying to locate her for goin' on four years now. How can I ever repay you?" Moses said as he shifted his gaze from Elise to Maya strangers he'd only come to meet and hardly knew and yet they'd accomplished something he'd been attempting for years in only a matter of minutes. He'd located mama.

"Where are you staying if you don't mind me asking, Moses?"

"I'm sorry. I have been so busy on the quest to find mama that I haven't even had the chance to think about lodging," Moses said now concentrating his gaze on Elise.

"We have that all arranged. He'll be staying the night with Buck or Phoenix while he's here," Elise said smiling.

It was obvious this was of a particular concern to both women and Moses excused him after thanking Maya again.

"Don't be so quick to thank me. I'll find the time for you to thank me before you leave tomorrow," she said grinning at Elise.

Yes. This was personal, and I wanted none of it so I excused myself and went outside and sat down and smoked while the two women talked.

Elise came out clearly disturbed.

"My God! That woman and I can't get along for anything. I try so hard but nothing I do seems to be good enough."

"Why does it matter so much what she thinks?"

"You don't understand Moses. It's like going to the queen for her blessing before you consider undertaking your journey. Her blessing could go a long way in securing a successful journey. She's not even considering our idea as reasonable or conceivable."

"And that idea being?"

"Much as I am enamored by your handsome presence and amenable ways I am afraid I cannot divulge that information to you Mr. Moses sir."

"You can tell that woman who does not care for your ideas and openly scorns you but you cannot divulge this plan of yours to one who lives on the run from the authorities."

"All that being said Mr. Moses there is a profound difference between yo and that woman."

"And what is that Miss Elise?"

"You are but a stranger Mr. Moses. That woman happens to be my mother."

Moses stopped in his footsteps.

"Your mother?"

"Yes. Miss Maya is my mother. There are fourteen of us running around here. All are massas kids so you see mama holds some power on this piece of land. She runs things when massas not here and a lot of time when he's here as well. He calls mama his right hand and makes no bones about us being his chi'dren. Gives mama anything and everything she could possibly want. Niggras are treated better hereabouts than anywhere else or so I am told and that's thanks to mama and her relationship with massa."

"Good Lord. This is a bit much to take. So, what you're telling me is that this Black woman has thirteen children by the owner of the plantation and is basically his wife and partner in all his fiscal ventures despite maintaining a white woman for appearances sake. But the woman who runs these twenty or thirty thousand acres is a Colored woman?"

"Yes. I do believe you've got it sir. A lil hungry Moses?"

"How can one think of food at a time like this. I hope someone has had the insight to record all this. Has anyone written this down. This is history. Oh, they'll absolutely love this in Boston. And they say that we are not equal in brain size and are mere animals. They say we are not capable and yet here is a Colored woman who is for all intent and purposes is running a huge plantation alone while her man and the father of her thirteen children is off fighting a war

to keep them enslaved. How ironic. Oh, what a story

this will make. The abolitionists will eat it up. This

my friend Elise is sensational news."

Elise hardly saw the big deal. She'd grown up

like this. It was normal to her, commonplace. She

knew of nothing else.

She left the man she had come to know as

Moses with Phoenix and Buck who shared a three-

bedroom cabin that had just now been finished after

close to two years of construction. To the two young

men it was perhaps the finest slave cabin ever

constructed. And to the many who came to view it

most agreed. It made sense now. No wonder there

was no urgency for them to leave this life that

afforded them a better lifestyle than the average, poor,

southern, white dirt farmer trying to eke out a meager

existence on a poor tract of land. And it was Miss

Maya who had the heart and soul of this white

landowner who allowed all this to happen here in the heart of Dixie right under the noses of men who despised any positive contribution of the niggra. And it had been under Miss Maya's tutelage and business savvy that she had elevated the McClowry plantation to one of the most lucrative and productive plantations in the state. Mr. McClowry was fully aware of the reason for his success and saw no reason to do anything to thwart Mayas's business prowess. But it was not Maya's business prowess that were solely the reason for the plantations success. No. There were other contributing factors that tied to the overall success. There was the fact that she rewarded those planters that brought in the biggest harvests. Instead of having one big field she let the men divvy up the land into fifty and seventy-five-acre plots and let the men compete against each other for the highest crop yield. She then gave permission for the men to keep everything they grew outside of massas take. And never had we seen such a bevy of activity as men worked feverishly to bring in the massa's take as well as their own and then enough to sell along the road side to gather some savings to flee North and begin a new life there. Others had no plans of leaving and were intent on building fine homes under Miss Maya's watchful eye.

"Listen people. We all come from the same place and yes, it's true that we as a people like nice things. After all, we are from either the Ivory Coast or the Gold Coast of Africa. How can we not help like the finer things in life? But we must not flaunt our good fortune in front of those less fortunate than we are. We must not bring attention to ourselves. We must remain humble under His watchful eye. So, I am asking you to be smart and those of you who have gone out on your own and turned your labor into a profit and are now thinking of providing a better home for your loved ones I only ask you to be modest and humble in your building. And if you choose to be lavish please do it on the inside of your home but do not let the outside draw attention. I hope this is understood."

On one such occasion when massa stopped by for a brief visit and saw the result of Maya's work he was elated but when she attempted to explain her management skills that made it all possible he purposely changed the topic of the conversation. Realizing this Maya also understood that despite his fondness for her and all her success in managing the McClowry plantation he still did not want to hear of her success. After all, it went against the very doctrine of the slave trade. Coloreds weren't smart enough to govern themselves let alone govern and successfully run a plantation of nearly five hundred slaves.

Maya chose to ignore the major's slight though and instead focused on having the major sign off on everything from the twenty new cows and two bulls she considered necessary to feed her people and share in the burden of the plowing. She also had him sign notes for ten, fifteen, and twenty thousand dollars. It had long been established that she handled all of the major's banking matters and being that he believed that she was not capable of either reading or writing there was little or no worry that she would or could forge any official documents. No, she was no more than the attractive, well-dressed niggra slave that the major trusted enough to use as a courier. Maya had been the major's courier for years now and there had yet to be an incident of any kind, so no one noticed her on this particular day when she sauntered in with three separate bank notes totaling forty-five thousand dollars.

"That's quite a lot of currency you're carrying there gal. Would you like me to send someone along with you?"

Maya wanted to cuss him. This young white boy posing as a bank manager calling a forty-year-old woman gal. She with thirteen children running and directing most of the white men in town under her wiles and acumen under the major's name and the best she could garner was gal. Yes, it was almost time to put her plan in play as well. And there was no time like the present before she had to kill one of these crackers for just not knowing any better or wanting to know any better. Perhaps her daughter Elise was right. Perhaps it was time to tae up arms and declare war on these heathens.

"Are you listening to me gal? Do you need me to send someone with you?"

"No, suh. Oh, look at the time. Oh, no sir. Let me go suh. Massa told me to come right back. I gots to go," Maya said bending down low and pausing just a moment to distract the young bank manager who gasped aloud. Grabbing the two satchels she was up on the carriage and off before the bank manager could regain his composure.

On the way back to the plantation Maya's mind was flooded with a plethora of problems. There was her daughter Elise the one most like her. Out of all her children Elise was not only the one most like her but the one that caused her the most anguish. Now she and her boys who some say acted as the protectorate and militia for the McClowry niggras was ready to enact some crazy scheme to level the playing field for niggras. There was no way these four could ever pull it off and Maya after discussing it with her daughter decided that the only thing Colored folk could do for they selfs was to educate and motivate their children so that their offspring would take the struggle forward and enhance the living conditions for their children.

If niggras did this, they would rise from the ashes to their true status of kings and queens once more. It would take time. This she had learned over the course of time. But Maya knew that if it's one thing that young people lacked it was patience. For Elise they had not suffered the full impact of the peculiar institution, but they—even at their young ages—had seen enough and could not afford to suffer the injustices anymore.

Maya's thoughts were not only concerned with Elise. Her main concern was with Elise's father who refused to acknowledge her as a human being comparable to any other because of her skin tone and gender. Sure, he was gracious in giving. He gave her anything he even thought she had an inkling for but to acknowledge her as his equal he just could not do.

Maya's thoughts quickly turned to the young man she'd had the opportunity of meeting the night before. Moses was his name and my goodness was he ever handsome. She'd promised to make him pay today and she felt herself warm at the thought of him.

Perhaps he hadn't left yet. One thing was for sure it was time to pay Gertrude a visit. But first she would stop by and invite the very handsome Mr. Moses to lunch. And she still had to check on her charges and just get a feel for things in general. Since the war the majority of her friends and family were ready to pull out and make a stake on their own. She had done her best to dissuade them. What would a few more months mean? They would at least be more prepared for the long journey ahead and although she understood their angst it made no sense leaving in the middle of winter for places unknown and as of yet untraveled with little or no supplies for as many of them that were going. At last count there were close to four hundred choosing to make the journey North. Most were no more than field hands, but their sheer numbers alone would make them less vulnerable than if they'd fled in small groups.

Still, most were farmers and even with their numbers they would be expected to protect themselves and their families. And so, Miss Maya put her own security detail in charge of training the men to shoot. Many were on their way to becoming crack marksmen under the tutelage of Elise, Buck, and Phoenix but all were at the very least ready to put up quite the formidable fight should it come to that.

Everything was in order although she knew it was a dangerous game she was playing. How long had she been shaving dollars off the McClowry plantations' books? Years. It had been years and he had yet to go behind her and check to see if she was accurate in her count. But neither had she withdrawn such a large sum. Her gut feeling told her that she'd gone to the well once too often, but they would need it going North. Maya knew the more money the easier the journey would be. Yet, there had been no word from the major in close to a month and if he were to stay true to form he should be returning home any day now. She hoped to be long gone by the time he arrived. With a skeletal crew of less than a hundred folks many of whom were sick or elderly the major would be hard-pressed to find a labor force in time to save the harvest. That, however was no longer Maya's concern. Her immediate concern was to get her people, her family as far away from the major's wrath as possible. And four hundred people traveling North was not got going to be easy to camouflage. Still, if they could at least cross the Mason Dixon Line they would have the federal government to defend them.

She'd left Killa in charge of making sure all that were going were up and ready to move by noon. They'd rehearsed their departure as well as the circling of the wagons at night in the event of any impending danger. They'd been ready weeks earlier, but it could never be said there was anything wrong with being overly prepared especially embarking on a journey such as this with so many folks.

Pulling through the gates of the McClowry's Maya breathed a deep sigh of relief. She was home—well at least as close to a home as shed ever known. Turning the big bay to the path that led through the quarters. Waving at her folks as she passed through one who didn't know one could easily think Miss Maya was some sort of famous person. A quarter of a mile past the quarters led a narrow trail into the woods. Following this some distance the woman came upon a fine-looking cabin. Out front sat the three men.

"Morning Miss Maya."

"Morning Buck."

"Morning mama."

"Morning Phoenix. Where are Killa and Elise?"

"They went to make sure the wagon train is ready."

"Good. Good. Its ten o'clock. The train will be pulling out at noon. Why are you two not helping them?"

"We're not sure if we're going mama."

"And that's fine. But that's not what I asked. My question is why aren't you helping the rest of your family get out of here?"

Both men dropped their heads.

"And I don't know where you're from Mr. Moses but people say good morning when they see each other for the first time each day. I am sorry this had to be an oversight on your part I am sure as you did say Gertrude was your mother."

"Yes ma'am."

"Then your lack of manners must certainly have been an oversight since I know my good friend

Gertrude would never have a son who would act in such a manner."

"No ma'am."

"Then place your hind parts in this here buggy. Hurry now. We have no time to waste. And Phoenix you tell Elise that this is it. I want you on the road at noon. If there are stragglers, then there just are. I don't know how long I've been pushing them for this day so if they're not ready to pull out at twelve sharp tell them to catch up. Don't wait on me either. I'm going to pick up my friend Gertrude. I'll be along directly."

"But mama don't you think you may need someone to ride shotgun?"

"Boy hush. I'm riding here with the good reverend who just so happens to be a free man and has been commissioned by Major McClowry to go round and preach to local niggras the importance of abiding by their massa's wishes and remaining on the plantation as they always have," Maya said smiling at her son.

"Now git," she yelled at the big, red, bay who responded to her voice lurching forward and nearly throwing Moses from his perch.

"I've come to the decision on a number of things where you're concerned Mr. Moses."

"Oh."

"Yes. As you can see we're getting ready to pull out. Headed North to freedom we are. Trying to get out of here before the good major returns and finds the majority of his livestock and food stuffs have been confiscated. What's going to really disturb the good major is that his labor force is gone. He gonna be mad as a wet hen and there's gonna be hell to pay. He depends on me to keep things in order and the niggras in line so he's gonna be out for my head when he finds that I led his niggras outta bondage," she grinned. "I'm thinkin' they should call me Moses."

Maya and Moses both laughed.

"Yes. I suppose he would be angry with you. From what your daughter tells me you singlehandedly supplied half of his labor force," Moses said dropping his head to conceal his smile.

"Oh no you didn't," Miss Maya said grinning. "I see you have a sharp tongue. Don't worry. I like a little spirit in a man."

"Seriously though Maya. You don't mind me calling you Maya do you?"

"No sir. Feel free. I have a feeling—call it a premonition—but before this day's over I have a feeling you'll be calling me a few things. By this time tomorrow I'll probably be happy if that's all you choose to call me," she said smiling sinisterly.

"What is it that you have in mind for me Maya? You've pretty much peeked my interest."

"A little fear and curiosity is not a bad thing. Be patient. The way I see it we'll stop by my place and have a little lunch followed by dessert and then we'll head for Atlantic Beach. The entire way to see Gerty I want you to familiarize yourself with the good book as you are the young preacher sent to speak to those heathen niggras about fleeing North. I am the older woman and a bishop in the church sent to escort you and make sure you are not distracted in your plight. Once we pick up your mother we will join up with my folks and you will lead us the safest way out of this God forsaken land."

"You have it all figured out don't you," Moses said glad to have the older woman's company on this trip. Still, and for some reason he couldn't exactly put his finger on he had his reservations when it came to his mother's friend.

"Whoa sugar! Whoa!" Maya said pulling on the reins and slowing the horse to a walk as she pulled up in front of her cabin. "We'll leave her saddled up," Maya said to Moses who was already unbuckling the harness.

"You sure?"

"Yes. We shouldn't be more than an hour. Well, that is unless something unexpected comes up," the older woman smiled.

Moses followed the woman into the house where they were met with the sweet smell of freshly made biscuits. Moses thought he smelled a ham and entering the dining area of the kitchen he was met with a pretty young woman.

"Morning sir."

"Morning ma'am," Moses said grinning at the attractive young lady several years his junior.

"Everything's ready mama. I'm going to go grab Dre and we're going to head for the train. They should either be leaving or just pulling out. Anyway, let me get outta your hair," she said grabbing her mother by the shoulders and hugging her tightly.

"And you make sure you look out for my mama mister. Anything happens to her and they'll be hell to pay. Do you hear me?" the woman said her gaze penetrating Moses. She was serious.

"I promise to take good care of her," Moses said almost apologetically although he had no reason to be sorry. It was this woman who had voluntarily joined his quest to find his mother. He hadn't invited her. And now he was responsible for her welfare?

Lunch was delightful, and Moses couldn't remember the last time he had had a meal this good. Following lunch Maya poured the two Mint Juleps and requested Moses' company on the veranda outside of her bedroom. A non-drinker Moses took a seat to the right of the woman and was amazed at the view which took in the vast expanses of land, fields and slightly off to the right in the background sat the big house. Moses sipped the Mint Julep and felt his demeanor shifting. He couldn't help but notice that between the house he'd spent the night at and Maya's house he couldn't recall in his thirty years on God's green earth he had yet to see niggras living so lavishly. Not even in his travels that included the homes of free niggras in Boston and New York had he seen niggras living so well.

Maya stared out over the vast expanse. She was quiet as well. Moses could only imagine what she was thinking. This amazing woman had spent who knows how many years on this place catering to the massa and bearing him fourteen children. This amazing woman had somehow through her feminine wiles, shrewd cunning and intelligence had manipulated a compromise between the massa and his five hundred slaves where if they brought him a profit then they too would profit. Both had profited beyond their wildest dreams thanks to Maya and even though she'd acquired the best of everything for her niggras when Lincoln announced the slaves were free they'd started packing. When massa asked her behind closed doors what the intentions of the McClowry Coloreds.

Maya McClowry lay there and with a straight face said 'John you have nothing to fear. Your children love you. You have been a good father and most, if not the rest, feel the same way. And I don't care what Lincoln done proclaimed we cain't get much freer than we is now, so you stop your worryin' John McClowry.'

The major knew that if it came from Maya's mouth it could be considered gospel and not another word was spoken on the subject again. She'd way laid his deepest concerns while at the same time plotting the best course for them to make their escape.

"I hate to interrupt you. You seem to be in deep thought."

"Just reflecting on my years here is all."

"Do you mind if I ask you a question?"

"Not at all. Ask away."

"I've had the opportunity to travel somewhat extensively along the eastern seaboard and been to the homes of free niggras as well as slaves and out of all the places I've had the opportunity to frequent I must say you niggras living on the McClowry place are living better than any of the niggras I've happened to come across."

"So, why is it that we feel the need to leave this place when chances are we are living as well or better than we may ever live again? Is that your question?"

"Basically," Moses said shaking his head and putting out his pipe.

"I thought so. Listen, we have a day's ride ahead of us. Plenty of time for talk but I have something else in mind to occupy our time right now," she said grabbing his hand and pulling him through the French doors and letting her dress fall to the floor.

"Okay Moses. This is not the place where you ask mother may I. As you can see I am quite ready for you to indulge me."

At thirty Moses was somewhat ashamed to say he had yet to be with a woman but he couldn't have written the script any better on this day. This amazing woman who had located his mother after him searching n vain for the past four years was asking for a few moments of his time in the bedroom. He was truly blessed. He hadn't met too many women that could compare to her stark beauty. Like her daughter she was uprooted royalty but as could be seen from what she'd built here that it was hard to deny Black royalty. And to think, she wanted him. Moses was glad be able to avail himself to the older woman or, so he thought.

An hour later he was begging her to stop. They'd come together so many times in the past hour that she'd rubbed him raw. Now in pain he cried for her to stop. Seeing the ripped flesh Maya left him in his own misery only to return minutes later with some type of poultice and a few wilted leaves that resembled spinach or kale. Gently she applied the poultice and gauze.

"I don't know how I'm going to explain this to your mother, but I think you may just have a certain usefulness in my life. Come on sweetie pie. Let's go. They tell me it's a day's journey, so we'll travel 'til it gets dark—too dangerous to be out there at night anyway—then we'll pick up at first light and head on in and pick up Gertie."

"Sounds good to me."

Maya gave the reins to Moses who in turn proved to be a very good horseman.

"Oh, I see you're a man of more than just one talent."

"Miss Maya you give me far too much credit."

"I think not. Remember I just spent an hour with you and I must applaud you. Of course, I've only been with one other man and it was never of my own choosing. For the first time in my life I know what intimacy is supposed to feel like. Excuse my bluntness Moses but this is like a revelation to me. All I can say to those who have given up hope that Jesus is alive and well and working on our behalf. Well, this I can tell the doubters. He is alive and well and has lessed me once again. This I know."

"You ain't never lied. Preach sista," Moses said agreeing in earnest. "Thanks to you Maya, I am going to see my mother for the first time in seven years. That in itself is a blessing. And then he sent me you in a whole 'nother light. He graced me with your beauty, and your expertise to show me the ways of love and intimacy. And then as if that's not enough she pays me the ultimate compliment by telling me that after giving birth to fourteen children that it is I who is the first to make love to her."

"That would be correct Moses," Maya said leaning her head on his shoulder.

"I hope you heal up by tonight. I think I'd like to revisit that special place before your mother joins us. Well, that is if you're of a mind to?"

Moses grinned broadly showing every one of his near perfect, pearly white teeth.

"I guess ours was just a brief interlude in our complicated lives."

"Why do you say that with such doom and finality?"

"Come on Moses. How do you think my best friend will look upon me. Sleeping with someone young enough to be my son and just so happens to be hers. How do you think my folks will look upon us? And then I don't know if you've noticed or not, but my daughter Elise has her sights set on you."

Moses did not respond. The two rode on through the afternoon in perfect silence. Maya thoughts were consumed with the fact that she'd finally found some happiness brief though it was. In the end she had to surmise that happiness was just not in the cards for her. God had put her down here for other things. She was to serve others less fortunate and unable to help themselves. And she resigned herself to this. This morning was a blessing, a gift, nothing more. And despite her wanting to revisit those feelings of closeness and warmth and intimacy she knew it was probably her first and last time with the very handsome and intelligent Mr. Moses X.

Moses' thoughts were consumed with the fact that he was once again a Colored man in the Deep South. His mere appearance made him stand out and when he opened his mouth they knew he wasn't from there. In their eyes he was just another one of them high falutin' niggas from the North comin' South to stir up trouble among the good niggas. Probably still preachin' that abolitionist shit about niggas having equal rights. That's the way most whites saw him.

He wondered if this was finally the end of his travels. Once he had taken his mother North safely would he be finished, or would he continue to travel back to lead niggras North.

He wondered if there was any way around Maya's words. What she said was true. There was no denying it but there had to be a way he could share time with this woman who so enamored him. He would find a way.

"The horses are tired Maya," Moses said breaking the silence.

"We're a few miles outside of Fayetteville. Have some friends that stay there. I'm sure they will provide us lodging for the night. A few minutes later, Maya took the reins and guided the team of horses leading them through some rough backroads until they pulled up on a modest two-story brick residency.

"Colored folks reside here?" Moses asked.

"No, lil white gal I grew up with in New O'leans. Relax. You're gonna love Sadie."

"Sadie. Sadie Hawkins is you here?"

'Oh, my goodness. Is that you Maya? Oh, my goodness I can't believe it's really you Maya. Come here and let me give you a hug. Damn, it's good to see you. I was just thinkin' about you the other other day. I said I wonder what kind of shit Maya's mixed up in now," the pudgy little white woman said hugging Maya tightly. It was obvious the woman had been a looker in her day, but time and misfortune had taken its toll.

"Sadie this is my friend Moses. Moses I'd like you to meet one of my oldest and dearest friends. Moses meet Sadie."

"He is quite the handsome devil. I do hope you're not letting all that talent go to waste Maya."

Maya laughed out loud.

"Lord you ain't changed a bit."

"And ain't going to. I likes Sadie Hawkins. I didn't always but I do now. And yes ma'am, you did pick a fine one there. I wouldn't mind a roll in the hay with him. What time you usually go to sleep Maya?" Sadie asked her eyes never leaving Moses."

"Girl, you is certifiable," Maya said hugging her friend again. "And yes, I have been training him although I don't know why?"

"You don't know why? Girl you were always a little prudish. With youth comes vigor and that vigor keeps us youthful. But what would you know about that? You ain't never really been up close and personal with no man. All you know about is functional pussy.

What you be tellin' that fat cracker, Maya? 'Oh, that's it major. Oh, that's good massa'. Then he say. 'Is it good gal?' To which you reply? 'Yes, sir massa. It's good. By the way massa, do you think it possible that I can get four sacks of flour and four sacks of corn and the mule to help with the plowing.' And he say, 'Sho' gal. Whatever you need. Now just focus and concentrate.' 'Oh, and before I forget suh, may I have the big, red, bay and the carriage and I won't bother you no more tonight. I promise suh.'

He's getting frustrated by this time and just says. 'Yes! Yes! Now come on Maya!' You just serviced the big house with that functional pussy and all you was doing is the same thing you been doing for the last twenty years taking care of your niggras and taking care of the plantation. But who's takin' care of Maya? You deserve some happiness girl. I don't know how you're keeping him but enjoy the hell out of him while you have him."

"I didn't know that was possible."

"What's that?"

"How someone I haven't seen in five or six years can summarize my life in sixty seconds."

"How'd I'd do?"

"On point as always."

"So, you are taking advantage of Mr. Moses?"

"I am, and I hope to."

"And afterwards you go to sleep?"

"Will you stop?" Maya laughed.

"C'mon! What's the harm? You're not in love, are you? Then what's the harm. I just want him to scratch my itch one time. Is it okay if he agrees after you o to sleep?"

"You're serious?"

"Dead."

"Then you handle your business after I'm asleep and there's no need for me to know what transpires once I'm asleep. By the way how's your father Sadie?"

"Passed away two years ago. Out there in the garden at damn near ninety. But you know papa. Never could sit still. Doctor say he had a massive heart attack."

"I'm sorry to hear that. Papa was a good man. I remember when the Klan would come down to the quarters late at night and papa would show up by his lonesome and confront them. I remember the one time he rode up and said, 'Tom Burnett, Jack Hardy. I know that's you Elgin. Half your face is sticking out. I believe you gonna need a bigger mask. Now you fellas take off them ridiculous masks and stop harassin' these people for no reason. Now git on home. And do you know they turned on their horses and headed home. He was both loved and respected and there won't many tougher than he was."

"And that's the way he was until the end. Just as ornery as ever. You had to be on your toes at all times or he'd get you. I miss him so much."

"I'm sorry. I know you do so tell me what have you been doing to keep yourself busy?"

"Eating as you can see," Sadie said rubbing her stomach. "The place does real well on its own and so I hire a few folks to plant and harvest and look out for them and they make sure that we have good harvest every year."

"That's what I'm talking about. Papa taught us that when we were kids. Take care of your own and they will take care of you. By the way where's Moses. I haven't seen him since we've been here. Did he even come in?"

"Yes Maya. Don't you remember introducing him?"

"That's right. Well, where the hell did he slip off to?"

"I don't know but you'd better find him. Ain't had nohing that sweet come 'round here in a while. Find that boy. I gots plans for him," Sadie grinned.

Maya stuck her head out the front door and was pleasantly surprised to find Moses asleep in the rocking chair on the front porch. She smiled then closed the door quietly.

"He's asleep. Don't make 'em like they used to I suppose. In an hour he went from a tiger to a cub. And I was still wantin' him when he came up lame. I just hope he heals before we pick up his mother."

"His mother?"

"Yes. It's complicated. You see his mother is one of my good friends. Lives two farms over. Anyways he come through looking for her and was so tickled that I knew her that he couldn't refuse me my desires. But like I said he came up lame. I fixed and put a quick acting poultice on it and I'm hoping that he'll be ready for another round tonight before we pick her up but the way he's sleeping now I kinda doubt it. Guess I was too much for him. But damn I'd been waiting so long to experience some good lovin' and Lord knows this young man who just happened to be a virgin is gifted and was just what the doctor ordered."

"I hear you Maya. Then you're just gonna have to work around his mama being your best frend. Ain't nothin' wrong with both mom and son loving you Maya. Nothin' wrong with that at all."

"I might just have to give that some thought. Thanks Sadie. Moses isn't the only one exhausted. Where am I sleeping?"

"Top of the stairs, first door on the right. And get your friend. Some of the good ol' boys ride by and see him sleepin' on this white woman's porch and he's liable to get lynched."

"You right. And he sure can't be of no use out there sleeping. Let me get him up to the room where he can be of some use."

Sadie laughed at her old friend.

"Just make sure you save me some," Sadie said. There was no sign of humor in her voice.

"Moses! Moses! Come get to bed. We need to get an early start tomorrow. And no, you can't sleep out here. Nice as it is. They'll lynch you if they find you sleeping out here in front of this white woman's house. Now come on."

A few minutes later Maya undressed Moses who did not complain.

"You gonna take care of me Moses."

"And how do you propose I do that?"

"Do it just the way you did it this morning Moses. Take me there. Take me to the Promised Land."

An hour later Maya screamed her last scream of the night.

"Moses darling, we will just have to find a way to continue our affairs without anyone knowing it, but I can't let you go. Lord knows I can't let you go?"

"I think the smile on my face answers that. I thought about it all the way here and I couldn't see how you could say no more with impunity after this morning. That second dose did it though," Moses said smiling.

"I have a favor to ask of you Mr. Conceited and I wouldn't be in the least angry if you declined."

"Let's not even think about declining or being angry. Whatever it is you need me to do I can do for you after all you've done for me Maya."

"Well, in that case, my friend Sadie thinks you're quite attractive and being stuck out here in the backwoods she doesn't really come into contact with many a man as handsome as you and well she'd like for you to bed her down. I know she's a little on the pudgy side, but she was once a beautiful woman. I guess you can see that."

"You don't have to sell me on Sadie, Maya. If this is what you want me to do, then I will do it."

"No. This is not what I want. This is what my good friend Sadie has begged me for all night while you were outside sleeping. But know I do not want to share my lover."

"Then why do it?"

"Because she is my friend. Can I send her in?"

"Send her in Maya but it is you who I want to spend my night with."

"Then I will return when you have exhausted her."

"Or I will come to you when she is sleep."

"That's fine m'love," Maya said getting up and wrapping the sheet around her before knocking on Sadie's bedroom door.

"Come in."

"I left you some," she said smiling at her childhood friend.

"No way I thought I'd see you anymore tonight. You are truly a friend'" she said rushing to get out of the room.

Twenty minutes later Sadie Hawkins was sound asleep a smile etched on her face. The following morning Maya and Moses were up and on their way at the crack of dawn. Sadie was still asleep when they left and Maya was tempted to drag Moses back to the bed but thought of Sadie who was intent on going with them changed her mind. It would have made good sense to take her along. It wasn't the first time she had escorted Maya somewhere posing as the mistress with her assistant in tow. But on her way to the outhouse last night she'd offered Maya the world to keep Moses. She'd become obsessed with him in the fifteen minutes or, so she'd spent with him. Maya had to smile. She understood which made it so much more important that they get out of there while she was still asleep, Sadie had always been treacherous when someone stood in the way of something she wanted. And she wanted Moses.

"Ten grand for the services of your man-child, boy-toy or whatever you choose to call him Maya. You know I'll cater to his every need and all he has to do is fulfill one of mine."

"Can we discuss it in the morning Sadie. Ten grand is a fair offer but right now all I want to do is pee," she recalled telling her friend in the wee hours of the morning. The Sadie she had grown up was liable to do anything and right now she had her sights set on Moses.

Once they had a good forty or so miles between them and Sadie's Maya could finally breathe a sigh of relief.

A young Black boy walked along the shoulder of the road.

"Pull up next to that young man." Maya instructed Moses.

"Excuse me sir," Maya said to the young boy who couldn't have been more than ten. "Excuse me sir, but do you know where an old married couple can get a room for a couple of hours."

"Miss Millie runs a boarding house and is always renting out rooms," the boy responded. "Want me to show you where it's at?"

"Oh my, would you be so kind as to?"

"Move over lady. You don't expect me to walk do you?"

Moses was forced to laugh.

"Where to sir?"

"Straight up. I'll tell you when to turn. Glad ya folks was coming along. Wasn't fittin' to make this walk but mama said I needed to go stay with my nana for a few days on account we ain't got no food."

"Why don't you have any food if you don't mind me asking sir?"

"First off, my name is Jeremiah, not sir and as far as us not having food it's simple. Mama cain't work the fields with her being with child and all and as everyone knows you don't work you don't eat. So, when we run out it's off to nana's for me."

"Well sir—excuse me Jeremiah—we are on our way North to Boston where there are plenty of jobs for boys just such as you. You are welcome to join us if you would like to. We will be back later tonight—like I said—if you should choose to join us. That way and after you get established you'll be able to send your mother money or come back and buy a piece of land for your folks."

"I'll think about it," he said as if the offer he was receiving he received every day. "Pull up in front of the yellow house. This is Miss Millie's. You don't need no introduction or nothing. What time do y'all think you'll be passin' back through?"

"I guess sometime between eight or nine. We'll be lookin' for you."

"Thanks," the boy said before hopping down and continuing on his way.

"Smart young man," Moses mused.

"Smart as a whip. Think he'll come back?"

"Don't know but he'd stand a better chance."

"All we can do is pray," Moses said following Maya to the door.

After a few minutes of knocking a rather stout, dark-skinned woman came to the door.

"Morning. May I help you?"

"Yes ma'am. My husband and I are on our way to Fayetteville and wanted to stop and rest for a spell and freshen up before heading in."

"Well, come right on in. And you are?"

"Maya McClowry and this is my husband Moses McClowry."

"You're not the same Maya McClowry that they say runs the McClowry plantation. There's a legend about this Colored woman who runs one of the most successful plantations in North Carolina."

"About that room."

"Ah yes. Right this way. But tell me. You is her ain't you? You's that famous Colored woman that runs the major's plantation. Is it true what they say that you have seventeen or eighteen kids by the major?"

"Woman did I not just introduce you to my husband? Does he look like he's old enough to have seventeen or eighteen children?"

"Well, no but they say you had them by the white major."

"The room please."

"Ah yes, that'll be one dollar."

Maya paid her and was glad to see her hind parts heading down the stairs.

"They say ignorance is bliss. She must be one helluva a blissful woman. Come here Moses. You know we're only an hour outside of Fayetteville," Maya said pulling Moses into her embrace.

"And your point is?"

"That this is the last time we can make love freely."

"As long as it's not the last time?"

"Never my love. I will die with you in my arms."

"Is that a promise."

"It is."

Neither could remember how many times they made love that day but when they awoke a bond had been formed and the rest of the world would somehow just have to find a way to accept it.

Arriving at the plantation at somewhere between nine and ten the two quickly found the quarters. After asking three or four people and all claiming not to know Gertrude Maya began to get the impression that the niggras had something to hide until they came across an elderly woman.

"Of course, I know Gertie. She was one of my dearest friends. I was a shocked as anyone when I heard she passed away."

"Passed away," Moses screamed. "When was this?"

"Gertie passed away. What's today?"

"Sunday."

"Gertie passed away Wednesday. We stayed up late Tuesday night just a talkin' and reminiscing then I wake up Wednesday and they tell me my girl is gone. Hurts like hell. Just goes to show you that no days are promised and ya better make the best of each one He blesses you with."

"You're so right," Maya responded crushed visibly by this latest news.

"She buried over here. Come on I'll show you," the elderly woman said. "She died natural though. Won't like she got whipped or beat. Nah.

Massa was very fond of Gertrude. Here she is," the woman said pointing to a crudely worked headstone that simply said Gertrude.

Maya and Moses were both speechless. Five minutes later, Moses took Maya's arm.

"Come on Maya. There's nothing else we can do here."

Maya followed Moses to the carriage. Helping her up he thanked the old woman before climbing into the carriage and grabbing the reins.

"Are we stopping back at the inn or you want to head back m'love?"

"Let's head back. We're a good three or four days in back of the wagon train. And I'm a little concerned about them and I'm sure they're worried about us. So yes, we should head back. Oh, and Moses I am sorry for your loss."

Leaning over he pulled Maya to him.

Three riders approached in the distance forcing Maya to sit up.

"Where y'all niggas headed in this fine carriage? Y'all uppity niggas ain't you? Hey Frank, look at the way these niggas is dressed."

"Hi falutin' niggas iffen you ask me. Dressed better than most of the white folk 'round here," the man referred to as Frank commented.

"Probably northern niggas. Let's bring 'em down a peg. Whatcha think Ross?" Frank said jumping down from his horse and grabbing the riding crop from Moses' hand."

"I don't think you want to do that. Major McClowry would be quite upset if anything were to happen to his Colored preacher."

"Oh, so you one of the major's niggas?" the man called Ross said as he circled the carriage and come to Moses who stared straight ahead careful not

make eye contact with the poor white trash looking
for some way to profit from the two finely dressed
Coloreds.

"Iffen we can get on with our travels we will
be sure not to mention to the major why we were
delayed," Maya said to Ross.

"Is you threatening me nigga?" the man
yelled.

"Do you have children sir?" Maya asked.

"Yeah, I got kids. What's that got to do with
the fact that we getting' rid to whip you and the
reverend's Black ass?"

"Because if you ever want to see those
children again you will take off your shoes and socks
put them in the back of the carriage and hand me the
reins to your horses."

"Nigga is you crazy," An infuriated Ross
yelled at the woman in front of him.

It was at this time that Maya with all the cool precision of a seasoned gunfighter raised her petticoats to reveal the sawed-off shotgun beneath.

"I believe I asked you gentlemen to remove your shoes and socks."

Five minutes later the three white men stood on the side of the road barely dressed.

"You cain't leave us out here like this with no clothes and no horses. The closest town is twenty miles away."

"You should have thought of that before deciding to accost innocent travelers along the road today," Maya said tying the horses to the back of the carriage.

"Nothin' worse than seeing po' white trash out here trying to rob po', helpless, Colored folks. Lord knows they made a mistake today? Just shoot 'em Maya and let's be on our way. You know you gonna end up doing it when they get likkered up enough to come back after these mangy ass horses."

"I really don't think they want to want to look down the barrel of Josephine twice in one day. The next time she might not be so charitable and forgiving."

"Praise the Lord," Moses said swinging up into the wagon to join Maya who had put the shotgun back in its place of concealment and hurried the horses along at a gallop.

"Quite an eventful morning," Moses mused. "That inn doesn't sound half bad at about this point."

"I wasn't thinking sweetheart. This must be an especially hard morning on you with Gertie and all. We can stop if you want to. Perhaps and if you're of a mind to you might find me to be a comfort to you in some way."

"Maya, I must admit that you are quite an amazing woman. I do declare I have never met anyone quite like you."

"I hope that's a compliment and I must say you are quite amazing in your own crusading right."

"I have to say though that I may have not handled matters in quite the same manner but then I have never been that quick thinking."

"Wasn't quick minded at all m'love. I loaded that gun in Fayetteville. Always gotta plan for the unexpected. I believe in praying for the best and planning for the worst. Always been like that. I don't know why but it's served me well up until now."

"Let me ask you something else, Maya. Why did it seem like we were running from Sadie's this morning? I never even got a chance to thank her for putting us up for the night."

"Chances are if you'd stayed to say goodbye you wouldn't have been able to leave. She met me in the middle of the night on my way to the outhouse and offered me ten grand for you. Told her I'd sleep on it. I'm afraid if I'd told her slavery was over it may have been the end of you and me. Sadie can be quite treacherous. Needless to say, we won't be stopping back by there. I'm surprised she didn't follow us. She wanted to ride along but I nipped that in the bud. I don't know what you gave her, but I want some of that," Maya laughed.

"And you call her your friend?"

Moses dropped his head and smiled. Old enough to be his mother he wondered if something was slight ajar. He'd even flirted with the idea of entering relationships on several occasions but had never followed through for this reason or that, but this was different. He had never had time to think. It had all happened so quickly. She'd seen him and that was it. She had been strong enough to demand his sex which he usually held in casual reserve but had yet to share with anyone. It was almost as if a twister had come along and gathered him up with all the winds and gusts to sweep him off his feet and he was none the sorrier for it holding on to one swiftly rushing gust after another. And just when he felt he could gather himself enough to see what was happening to him she would pull him back into a world that had been all but forbidden up until now. It was joyous, this ride. Moses hoped it would never end but he was not in control. Never had been.

"Impregnate me Moses."

"What?!"

"Make me with child, Moses."

"Are you serious? Why would you want me to impregnate you?"

"So, whatever happens to you or me I will always have a part of you."

They made love until both were spent before holding each other until they were both asleep.

In the morning they were back on the road. Maya armed with shotgun and a small pearl handled pistol that stayed in her clutch on her lap.

Moses grinned glancing the gun in the half-opened bag as riders approached.

"I'd hate to get you on my bad side."

"Self-preservation is the first law of nature."

"I've heard that said."

Three older Colored mens passed by on mules. Each nodding as they passed.

"Now you see that's how neighborly folk pass on the road. And they say we ain't civilized."

"When it comes to money white folk will rob their mama's for a dollar. I seen it happen. I see it every day with Missy McClowry taking a few thousand here and there from her husband's account. And why she do it? Not cause she need it but because the opportunity presented itself. No other reason. The major know it. He know it, but I don't believe he'd ever call it to her attention.

Funny thing is he has so much guilt when it come to her that he would give it to her if she'd just ask but that's not why she takes it. She takes it because she thinks he doesn't know but most of all she takes because white folk is greedy and they evil to the core. She could have the whole kitten caboodle if she just sat down and thought about it. But her greed stands in the way so instead of having all of the McClowry Place at her feet she settles for enough to buy a new dress here and there."

We rode on now and I wondered what other thoughts Maya had and what made her so different from the white Mrs. McClowry. She too had seized the opportunity and had traded in all of her wares to procure a comfortable lifestyle for she and her charges. So, what made her so different? It was too soon to ask but over time I was sure she would enlighten me.

Over the next two days I learned far more than I ever expected to learn about Maya McClowry. She told me how she'd been brought up in the French quarters of New Orleans and learned to fire a gun at a very young age. By the time she was twelve she was being entered into marksmanship competitions she'd become so proficient with her knowledge of guns.

Growing up in the quarters she learned to become proficient at far more than firing guns and along with Sadie and a couple of other friends began robbing the wealthy white planters who visited New

Orleans on every occasion. When they weren't

robbing the slaveowners they posed as domestics and

cased and robbed some of the richest residences in

New Orleans. When the pickings were scarce most of

the all-girl gang turned to prostitution, but Maya had

never seen this as an option. Being frugal, Maya

saved most if not all of her money from the break-ins

and robberies and was never what you might call 'in

dire straits'. But when the gang was finally caught

she was hired out to Major McClowry who was

enamored by the very, bright and beautiful Maya.

From the beginning, she'd had a spell on him that in

the eighteen or nineteen years they'd been together

had yet to lessen. He would have a hard time

admitting it, but he loved this woman, his slave, his

concubine.

And after observing the major for close to a

year and how he had a penchant for everything that

called him away he had far less enthusiasm for the

ordering of stock, the actual tilling of the soil or keeping of the books. These responsibilities now fell to Maya who showed not only confidence but a proficiency unheard of with numbers. In only a manner of months after he put the elegant young Colored to the task of handling the books the McClowry Plantation went from being in the red to being in the black.

Major McClowry could now go on his frequent forays knowing the plantation was not only in good hands but was actually prospering. On occasion he would suggest that she accompany him in order to see new places and broaden her horizons. At first Maya had taken advantage of these forays wanting to see both Richmond and Washington but the fact that she was viewed as this white man's concubine truly disturbed her and so she declined any future offers.

"You know what used to bother me most about the whole thing?"

"What's that sweetheart?"

"The fact that they don't look at us as people. I don't know how many times folks has come to visit the major and I'm serving them brandy and cigars and some ol' shriveled up cracker owner will turn to the major with one eye still on me and say, 'Say major what would you take for that rather comely wench serving us tonight? They was referring to me of course. Major would always say 'no'. 'That that one's not for sale gentlemen. I have some other wenches that would serve you right though iffen you're just lookin' to warm your bed for the night."

"Just like that?"

"Just like that. Almost as if we won't people. That right there used to tear me up. And after they inquired about me he would have the gall, the unmitigated gall to give me a list of the women—

married or not—so he could parade us in front of

some crackers, so they could choose who they would

bed down that night. Didn't matter what we thought.

Our say didn't matter. We didn't have no say. What

it was was legalized rape. They write the laws. We

didn't have no say."

"But we can respond. There are so many

ways in which we can respond."

"We are responding now," Maya smiled.

"Yes. Retribution can be devastating. The

major will be aghast when he finds that niggras who

he treated better than any niggras I've come into

contact with just got up and left him holding the bag.

He'll be seeking retribution of his own. Your sin is

that you niggras are ungrateful. What he may never

see is the horrifying conditions you were forced to

live under. But then he must first see you as human

and so many do not see us in that light. It would be

difficult to see us as anything other than slaves and concubines if they are to keep their current prominence."

"I do so enjoy talkin' to you Moses X. Makes me hot," she said grinning and hugging him at the same time. "I don't run into many handsome, Colored men as free-thinking as yourself. Guess the exposure allows you to think outside of the box a bit."

"I suppose. Didn't realize my thinking was outside of the box though."

"I'm sorry. Colored mens around here don't have many thoughts aside from how many bales of cotton they brung in today and will a couple of bushels of pole beans get me into your pants. There's not a lot beyond the immediate."

"You must have felt trapped."

"There were times I did but I tried to stay focused. What I wanted was outside of the realm of the McClowry place and so I came up with a plan, so we could all get a lil taste of freedom before we meet St. Peter at the pearly gates.

So, while Miss McClowry was providing my cover and she was content to rob her husband for a thousand here and there I was robbing him for tens of thousands at a time."

"Are you serious?"

"How do you think I funded this trip? Come on Moses. Did it never occur to you where the money came from to fund four hundred niggas on a trip North?"

"I just thought that under their living conditions that they all had their own."

"Many do. I've always stressed them saving for just such a day as this. And like I said many have a nice little nest egg to help them get established. But I'm their insurance in case things don't work out as planned. Always gotta plan for the unexpected. We have plenty of food stuffs, guns and ammunitions, new horses, livestock and a tidy amount of petty cash just in case I've forgotten something. All this with the blessings of the major."

"My God woman, how long have you been planning this?"

"Since the first day that that man laid a hand on me," Maya said taking the reins from Moses. "You get some sleep, so you can take over in a few hours. Way I figger it we should be no more than a day behind them."

"Excuse me but I don't believe I was finished. So, and if you don't mind me asking how much cash have you accumulated since you started?"

"Not nearly enough. I have some rather lofty goals. Our folks need a school; a church and things of that nature and these things do not come cheaply."

"No, but here's a proposal for you. We purchase a piece of timberland, fifty or sixty miles outside of Boston where land is cheap, and we let the men cut the timber. Then they will deliver it to our lumberyard where we'll sell it for a significant profit. We employ the men and allow them to purchase the land with small subsidies being taken from each of their paychecks. This way you keep the community together, prospering and intact."

"That's all well and good Moses but I know little or nothing about lumbering."

"That's it. I know everything thing there is to know about the lumber business. I grew up in a lumber yard watching my daddy run it for Massa Henry. I learned it all and before I began my forays South I ran a small lumber yard on the southside of Boston. White fella who owned it didn't know much about the business but when he saw that I did he dropped it all in my lap. Paid me handsomely too.

Would have still been there if I didn't get the itch to run South and look for mama," Moses grinned.

"Right. Who runs South although I am glad that you did," Maya said resting her head on his shoulder. "But you're sure this lumberyard will work?"

"I've seen a few men with a little knowledge grow rich. It's hard work but it's honest work. And I know of no other that can employ so many at the outset and what our folks are going to need first and foremost are jobs."

"Sounds like a plan to me Mr. X. Now please go to sleep so you can take us through the night. I do believe we should meet up with them early, tomorrow afternoon."

"You're anxious to meet up with them. Have you grown tired of me already?"

"Oh no silly. It's just that with all this talk of money I would feel better if I were there with the money. As it is no one knows it even exists let alone that there's close to two hundred and fifty grand within their midst's."

"Two hundred and fifty grand?!"

"You were a busy something weren't you?"

"Over twenty years and considering the millions I made him. That's really no money."

"I guess you're right. No wonder it was so easy to turn your girl down when she offered you the ten grand."

"Had nothing to do with money Moses. I wouldn't have entertained that offer if I'd been flat broke."

"And why is that?" Moses asked continuing to bait the pretty woman sitting to his right. He too had not engaged in conversation such as this in eons.

"Because no matter how good a friend she appears to be she is still white and though she is fond of me she still sees niggras as commodities. She expected me to grab that money and head out before you woke that morning but the days of buying and selling niggras is over in my eyes and I was more than a little offended by her proposition."

"I sensed that."

"Now would you please go to sleep sir?"

"I think I will take a nap. This has all been a bit much for me to take in."

"You asked," Maya said smiling. "You let me know if I'm a might much for you, you hear?"

"Just another new challenge," Moses said before closing his eyes and drifting off to sleep.

Be at a loss

Be at a loss

BOOK II

I'm not sure how long I slept but it was well into the night when I awoke.

"We made good time. Can you make out that dust storm up ahead?"

"Barely."

"That's them. I beat all to hell and am not in favor of sleeping outside after that ride. Passed a sign that said Charlottesville about a quarter mile back. Why don't we get us a good night's rest and join them lookin' like new money in the mornin' and ready to lead them out of Egypt."

"Sounds good to me. Any alone time with you is fine with me."

Maya smiled. She liked this man. Lying in his arms later that night she turned to Moses.

"Let me deal with my daughter in the morning. She's going to be quite upset at what has transpired since we last saw her. I ain't sure about you but I haven't felt this way—why come to think of it—I have never felt this way. And I have only you to thank for making me happy."

Moses pulled her to him.

"I have learned so much from you in so short a time. I have been the one that has been blessed."

"Then let us get these people North so we can begin our lives Moses."

"We will start out at first light."

True to his word Moses made enough noise to awaken the entire camp.

"Let's go people. Daylight is a wastin'. Don't you want to get out of this foul land that has beaten and enslaved you. Let's go people. Let's go breathe some of that northern air. They say it smells of freedom."

"Then we are right on your heels," one man yelled throwing his bedding in the wagon before harnessing his team of horses and jumping into his wagon. Most of the other folks seemed motivated by the good-natured jousting compliments of this stranger and their new leader. Maya's presence eased what tension there was, and the wagon train moved out a lively pace and it wasn't until noon—around six hours later—that Moses slowed the caravan down to a walk. Even Maya wondered where he got the strength from after pushing this same team of horses for three straight days.

"I know it's rough on a lot of them but not nearly as rough as if McClowry caught up with them.

About fifty miles up we're going to cut through the Cumberland mountains of Maryland. Takes three or four more days but there's still ice and snow up there. McClowry won't think we'd go that way and even if he knows we did he won't follow us up into the mountains. And it's slow traveling through the mountain passes so we need to make time while we can. We don't want him onto us just as we are reaching for something larger than the life he is offering us."

"Then let's be on our way. I think everyone's had a chance to catch their breath," Maya said.

Moses smiled.

"Give them another minute or so massa," Moses said smiling. "Have you even seen your kids?"

"They know where I am at all times. They'll be around when they have a might to. They're very strong and independent. You'll see. I raised them to be that way. I was never really worried about them as I am bandits that could have looked at this wagon train as a gold mine. And although they're trained many have never been tested under fire."

"Well, that may all be coming to an end real soon," Moses said taking out his spyglass and looking at the dust rising in the distance. Handing the spyglass to Maya he hurried about the half mile of wagon train.

"Circle the wagons. Quickly now! Circle the wagons and man your positions."

Suddenly, the cry went up through the camp and folks did as they'd rehearsed. Minutes later the wagons were in a tight circle and men and women armed to the teeth manned their positions.

"Who are they?" Maya asked.

"Have no idea. They're in uniform though. Not confederate though. Might be local militia. Could be your boy though. Rounded up some local toughs posing as militia to come look for you. I could probably get a pretty hefty sum if I sold you back to the major," Moses said grinning at Maya now.

"And I'd hate to have to put a load of buckshot in your pretty behind."

"Okay. Hold steady and don't fire until they do. Don't want anyone to say we provoked them. Hold your fire," Moses yelled as the horses bore down on their position. "Hold your fire."

A burst of gunfire broke the silence.

"Fire men," Moses yelled.

A steady staccato of fire rose from the wagons and men fell from their horses writhing in pain. After two more passes there was an eerie silence and a man on a horse came in under a white flag.

"Is everyone okay?" Moses yelled. A resounding yes came the refrain and Moses breathed a sigh of relief. Who was this attacking them for no apparent reason? He could only imagine. If a single niggra posed a threat how must five hundred moving without some white man in charge have appeared.

"Hey ma," Elise said walking up to her mother and embracing her. She was soon followed by Alexis the one who had cooked them lunch and threatened him around her mother's welfare. Phoenix was next with several others he had yet to meet.

"How we doing ma?" Elise asked.

"I'm not sure. We're about to find out though."

"Halt! Right there. Now speak your piece. Where are you from and who are you with? Why are you attacking us?"

"Is Miss Maya there?"

"This is Miss Maya. Who do I have the pleasure of speaking with?"

"It's Scotty ma'am."

"Oh, Scotty. Lower that silly flag and come in."

The man got down from his horse and walked towards the wagons which had now opened to allow him in.

"Scotty," Elise said smiling before hugging the white boy not much older than she. "The war's over so why are you in this silly uniform?"

"Papa came home and found y'all gone and lost his mind. Rallied the men up at O'Toole's. Bought a few rounds and started talking about how the niggra was ruining all that good white folk had worked so hard for. Then he started talkin' about organizin' a militia to protect the good white folks and keep the niggas in order. His words not mine.

Put me in charge and told me to hunt you and bring you back. If you was to refuse I was to kill every last one of you."

"Well, you take your dead and wounded back to him and tell him it wasn't as easy as he thought it was going to be and next time we will finish the carnage," and with that said Elise hugged Scotty as did Phoenix and the rest of the family. After all, the young man was their step brother even if the major didn't recognize it.

"I'll tell him although I doubt that he'll get it."

"Nevertheless, you did your job. Is there anything else?"

"Yes. I'm sorry Miss Maya," he said drawing the Colt 45 revolver. "But the rest can remain and go on with their journey, but I am to bring you back."

"Don't think that would be a good move my young friend. You see I've become quite enamored by Miss Maya and anyone trying to make her do something she wasn't exactly fond of doing I do believe I'd have to kill them. Now if you'd hand me your gun you can be on your way."

The young man turned around to find Moses, Henry repeating rifle aimed at his mid-section.

"They tell me there's nothing worse than being gut shot," Moses said to the younger white man.

"You know papa's not gonna be happy about this Maya," the young man said handing his pistol over to Moses but keeping his focus on Maya.

"Tell your papa that slavery is over, and he does not own me anymore. I am on my way to start a new life."

"I will tell him," he said hugging her before making his leave.

Once he was gone, it took us no more than fifteen minutes to reassemble the train and get back on the road. It was at this time Alexis rode up.

"I told you when you left to take care of my mother or else. Well, Mr. Moses I see that you are capable of doing just that. When we get settled I'm going to fix you a delicious meal," she said smiling before turning and riding off.

"I think I like her," Moses said grinning.

"I do so hope you two get along. She's the meanest of the lot."

"We'll be fine. You just watch. She and I want the same thing. Maya's happiness. How is she at soldiering?"

"She's a crack shot but like I was sayin' befo' ain't had no chance to see 'em soldier. Of course, she and her brothers and sisters went behind the lines for the Union and pulled off some raids. They all returned safely so I guess they are proficient. As my children I wouldn't expect for them to be anything but."

"And you say she's meaner than a rattler on a hot, sunny day?"

"She can be."

"May I speak to her?"

"Go get your sister. Tell her I need to see her now."

"Which one?" A pretty, little, caramel, girl of about five or six asked with adoring eyes.

"Alexis sweetie," Maya said bending down to kiss the child. The small child was elated with her mother's show of affection and dashed off among the wagons in search of her older sister.

"How old is Alexis?"

"Let me see Elise is twenty-one which makes Alexis nineteen."

"Do you think she can force the stragglers to keep up? If they continue to lag behind they make for easy pickings and we'll be forced to fall back and help them. But if I can put Alexis and she can make them stay close and arm her with three or four crack marksmen we may not even have to stop progress if we're attacked from the rear."

"I like the way you think but why not have crack marksman at different intervals, so we're protected at every point and never be vulnerable."

"Don't know your personnel Maya. Didn't know you had that many crack marksmen."

"Over a hundred."

"And who is currently running, training and responsible for guiding this train?"

"Why you are Moses. None of us has ever had the occasion to travel North. Why do you ask?"

Moses dropped his head and smiled.

I guess what I'm trying to ask is who was leading the wagon train before

we arrived?"

"Oh, that would have been Elise with the help of Buck, Phoenix and Killah."

"Then I want those four to be in charge of four different parts of the train going forward. Tomorrow we'll head into the mountains and we'll need to be tight and move with considerable speed. You know the militia will be back."

"Take them about twelve days to make the return trip and in those twelve days we have to prepare for them we should be dug in and ready for an all-out skirmish."

"We should be, but I didn't know you wanted to fight them. I thought our intentions were to get North with as little confrontation as possible?"

"It is but you don't know this man the way I do. The entitlement mess has got to go. We have been freed by the president of the United States and he has no claim unto me according to the law, but he keeps on. He needs to be stopped once and for all Moses. He has to be stopped," Maya said raising her voice on the way to becoming irate.

"Whoa! Slow down baby! I didn't know it meant that much to you. If it meant that much to you, we could have left a few good men to do away with him permanently on his return."

"Oh, no Moses I don't want to harm anyone. My reward comes in helping my people to a better life. But if he insists on forcing me to return then I think it is high time we eliminate any threat from him. In all honesty Moses, I'm tired. I'm tired of this cracker thinking he owns me. And now I can defend myself and eliminate him and all memory of him."

"I understand. And we can take care of that when the time presents itself but for now let's get everyone together and see what we can do to insure that we will be ready when they or anyone else poses a threat. Can you summon Phoenix, Elise, Alexis, Buck and Killah."

"It's done. And even though I share your enthusiasm for getting through the mountains do you realize that we have no time to share."

"I've considered that."

"And it doesn't bother you?"

"Sure, it does but I have no solution until we get to our destination."

"I can't wait that long m'love."

"Then what do you propose?" Moses asked.

"Charlottesville is about ten miles back. We can ride back and get a room. We can give the train a day off and be back by tomorrow night."

"Much as I would like to, I think we need to keep it moving to make sure we're out of danger."

"Oh, I hate you for always doing the right thing. Let me call the kids."

Within a half an hour all were assembled. Elise sat around the small campfire her gaze fixated on Moses. Moses tried his best to ignore the young woman when Maya interrupted.

"Our guide Moses has brought it to my attention that although we fought admirably against McClowry's militia that we are not yet a cohesive unit and are moving far too slow. We're about to head through the mountains which are treacherous with the snow melting and all. But this way makes it nearly impossible to ambush and attack us. What I'm going to need you four for is to tighten up our military presence. I need you to keep your sharpshooters sharp and on top of things. Each of you will be responsible for your portion of the train. And if you're smart you'll keep it competitive with your group competing against the other three each night in shooting and hand-to-hand combat. This should keep the men motivated as well as honing their skills."

Killah and the others smiled at the idea of leading a group and competing against each other.

"Just to add to that, I'd like to see the marksmen or snipers on guard in rotating shifts to make sure that we are protected at all times. What I want is these men on guard 24/7. Put your best people up front and out there in the times you see us most vulnerable. The rest I want trained on how to pull off a raid. We're going to use guerilla tactics and hit them when they least expect it. I need four groups of guerilla fighters. And I want them—better yet—I need them to be combat ready within a week. We can expect to see that same militia unit that attacked us earlier in about two weeks or when we should be coming out of the mountains and that will be fine. We'll send the rest forward and keep the militia occupied with just the four groups of guerilla fighters and our snipers. I'm trusting you four with their overall preparation. Good luck. If there are any questions, feel free to come and see me."

It was no surprise that Elise was the first to come see him.

"You didn't even come by to speak when you got back. I guess after being with the queen I was no more than an afterthought," Elise said grinning at Moses.

"Afterthought? I never gave you any kind of thought. Sure, you're mesmerizing and you took my breath away when we first encountered but I saw little more than that. And certainly, little reason to give you some thought," Moses grinned.

"Oh, you're feisty. Gotta little backbone I see. I likes that. I might find some use for you yet. But I guess you're right. I didn't have time enough time to get to know you. And I was so busy trying to help you that it was I who fed you to the jaws of the lion to be teased, squeezed and pleased before you were totally consumed. You don't have to tell me. You're still trying to figure what it is that has transpired between you and this woman. Like I said you don't have to tell me. I know mother. It didn't dawn on me how my plan on helping you would backfire. But I knew as soon as I brought you before her. I knew something was awry because I've never seen mother act that way before any man. But I've never seen her this happy and, in a way, it makes me happy to finally see her happy. You know I don't know if you know it or not, but she's really taken over by you. It must be something you're revealing

behind closed doors because you're not much in the

way of looks or personality now that I get a closer

look at you. Yes, it must be some secret talent behind

closed doors. But that's not to say that I'm not

curious and won't test your loyalty to her over the

next couple of months. What is they say Lucius?"

she said rubbing the big sorrels mane. "May the

winner take home the spoils," she said laughing

before jumping on the big, black, sorrel and trotting

off.

Moses had to smile. Any other time he would

have been flattered by the interest Elise had shown

but she was right he'd been struck by a force he'd

never known before.

"You spoke to them about what is was you

wanted and expected from them?"

"In general. I think they'll shore up

everything right nice. I'll talk to them individually

once I get to know their strengths. But yeah, I think they'll be fine for now."

"I saw Elise pull you aside. Everything okay?"

A steady beat of rifle fire arose from the rear of the train. Both Moses and Maya grabbed their horses and raced to the sound of gunfire. From the dust at the rear of the train one would have sworn it was the seventh cavalry. Moses held Maya back.

"Let her handle it."

A fairly large group of men dressed in Klan gear had appeared unexpectedly and out of nowhere firing into the air to frighten the niggas but who only incensed the bad-tempered Alexis who'd been napping.

"My goodness! What's all the commotion?"

"Looks like the local Klan done found some new niggras to mess with," Phoenix said.

"These ain't the ones. Where are they?"

"Behind that cluster of rocks," Phoenix said showing his sister.

"How many?"

"I'd say no more than ten or fifteen."

"Can we take them with just us and the snipers?"

"Yeah, c'mon it should be fun."

Alexis was quick to get her troops together and with the cover fire from the snipers keeping the Klan pinned down Alexis and her troops were soon upon them and had them circled.

"You can choose to fight it out or you can take your po' drunk asses home. Your choice," Alexis said to all within earshot. Seconds later despite objections a few horses and riders headed out.

Those that remained encountered a blistering round of rifle fire that sent up screams of pain and agony that saw a white flag soon follow.

"We should cut the rest of these crackers down for just being too stupid to leave when given the opportunity."

"Not today baby sister. The good Lord will look favorably on you for showing mercy."

"The good Lord is not a big fan of stupidity from what I've heard big brother," Alexis said smiling at her older brother. "So, tell me, what do you think of Moses?"

"Don't know. Haven't had a chance to really sit down and get to know him but mother's crazy about him and he seems preoccupied with her. She seems happier than I've ever seen her, so I guess he's good for her."

"I lik him. He's strong. Did you see the way he stood up to Scotty? Wouldn't have even known he was there until he threatened mama. I like that. I respect that."

"C'mon. let's ride through camp and see how everyone's doing."

"You go ahead. I'll catch up. Let me check my post."

"Mama. Moses. What are you doing here?"

"Heard the gunfire. Thought you may need our help."

"No. Just a few drunken, rednecks who thought they'd frighten some niggas. I think they were the ones that got shook tonight though," she said smiling.

"Anyone hurt?"

"None of us. I think a few of them are nursing wounds because of their own stupidity. I gave them the opportunity to go home. Some did. The smart ones did but then there were those stubborn, redneck—no nigga could ever beat me, crackers— that was surrounded and outgunned who still wanted to fight but you know some buckshot meetin' with a fresh white ass will change your mind right fast," Alexis grinned. "Not smart to leave the front of the train to ride back here though. If I heard correct my orders were to guard the rear. I don't believe I need someone to watch over me to do that," she said before riding off.

"Told you she was a mean ol' critter."

"Doesn't matter. She's as good as any a lieutenant I seen in the war and right now that's what matters."

"So, I guess after this little episode there's little or no chance of us sneaking away on our little, secret. rendezvous?"

"That's your call Maya but should those men come back the weight is on your shoulders."

"And I'd never be able to live with that. You're right. Let's get back and focus on the task at hand. We have a lifetime to sneak away. I guess I was being selfish, but Lord knows I miss that good lovin' you give me."

"We could always sneak away down by the river in the middle of the night."

"And what? Take a chance at some black snake crawling up in something? I think not. I guess I'll just have to wait until we reach our destination," Maya said sighing softly.

Moses dropped his head and smiled.

A week and a half passed and traveling though hard and slow moving through mountains they had not been threatened or fallen under attack. Moses was especially impressed by his fellow travelers. He hadn't known a whole lot of niggras in his time being up under his mama's apron things when he was young then shuttled off to the North when his mama had saved enough for him to attend normal school. His classmates were all-white, and it wasn't until he was a man and had completed his education that he decided to go and visit his mother that he was introduced to being a niggra or better yet nigga. This was about the time that President Lincoln decreed that he would allow niggra troops join the war effort at which time Moses signed up for the all Colored regiment out of Massachusetts. I believe it was the 54th. He made a formidable soldier and quickly rose to the ranks of Sargent Major.

But here in Maya's camp with her folks he came to know a people he had never known or encountered. These were literate niggras with a variety of skills all introduced and honed by Maya. And although they were purposely kept in the dark around their own conditions and the news of the day they were surprisingly well informed despite the efforts to the contrary.

"Knowledge means growth and we have quite the library if any of you would like to read before going to sleep. You that are masons who may want to read up on the latest in masonry I have something for you. The same for you that are brick masons and carpenters. Trust me my good friends, we have something for all your required tastes," Maya announced at dinner that night. "So, spread the word."

It was this Maya who used her bully pulpit to introduce news to her niggras as well as motivate them to become more than they presently were. At night after an unusually hard day of just walking the children were required to attend their own little makeshift school the same way they were at the McClowry's. You see Maya had this idea that not only were Coloreds as good as white folk they were better. After all, these were descendants of those that had endured and survived the Middle Passage.

"Got something up ahead. Not exactly sure what it is but it wasn't here the last time I was here," Moses said riding in at a gallop.

"What are we talking about?" Maya asked.

Hearing the commotion Elise came riding up.

"Everything okay?"

"I'm not sure but I don't think so. Put everyone on alert until we can get an accurate scouting report."

"Okay. I'm going to take twenty men out with me and see what's going on."

"You be careful Elise."

"I'll be fine ma," she said summoning her troops and then riding off in the direction Moses had come from. No more than a half an hour later. Elise rode back into camp.

"Hillbillies blocking the road. Says it's his land and there's a dollar toll to pay for each person and animal crossing his land."

"He armed?"

"To the teeth. He and his seven sons are all carrying shotguns and revolvers."

Moses turned to Maya.

"You already know my answer to that." She said shaking her head.

"Okay. Well, that settles that. Elise what would you say is the best course of action?"

"I think a show of force should be enough to change this cracker's mind. A hundred-armed men should make him rethink this whole toll thing."

"Then let's run with it," Moses said smiling at an approving Elise. "Do you want me to come along?"

"Been doing this long before you came along," Elise said smiling before she turned and rode off.

"That girl's something," Moses said looking at Maya.

"She's the child closest to me in temperament. Good natured but very independent. And smart. Right now, she's baiting you. Just be careful she doesn't lure you in."

"Can't see that happening. I've always been one to prefer the original and once I have that why search for anything else?"

"I kinda like the way you think Mr. Moses X. But how can you turn away from someone so young and beautiful."

"As I said before, age before beauty. With age comes wisdom," he said pulling her forward and between the wagons before kissing her deeply passionately.

"Oh, now why did you have to go and do that?"

"I had no choice. I guess I was overwhelmed by your beauty. Don't fault me for falling in love with you."

The smile quickly left Maya's face.

"Did I say something wrong?"

"No, Moses. You didn't say anything wrong," she said holding her head down.

"I did, didn't I? I'm sorry but I'm feeling some sort of way when I'm around you. I have never felt this way before in my life and it feels wonderful. So, the only thing I can attribute it to is the fact that I'm falling in love with you."

Glaring up at him Moses knew he had hit a nerve.

"Listening to what you're saying. Up until now you'd been everything one could have ever hoped for but are you hearing what you're saying? I know men that say 'no ready-made families'. That means if there is even one child they won't date you. And in some ways, I understand. I don't have one child I have fourteen. I am twelve years your senior and have children damn near your age. The way I see it we are doing the best we can and that's good enough for me. But no. Now you want to bring another variable into the equation. Love. Isn't that the word you used? What is that? What the hell is love? Is that the same love my mother told me as she pushed me into Major McClowry's wagon. Wonder how much she got for me but that's neither here nor there. The other time I heard the word love was when the major was fittin' to go up in me. So, you see when someone says they love me I'm ready to go and get my pistol."

"I didn't know but when I tell you I'm falling in love with you believe me. I just hope you're falling for me too."

Before Maya could respond there was gunfire. Moses began to run for his horse when Maya grabbed him by the arm.

"You do remember the last time you went charging off."

Moses found a hollow log and dragged it over to the fire. Sitting on the log and pouring himself a cup of coffee he had to be content to wait. It seemed like hours since they'd heard the first volley and still there was no word.

"Don't worry sweetie. Elise is thorough. Probably just supervising the burial retreat and covering up any evidence. Those in the party that don't know what transpired tonight won't be able to tell what happened tomorrow and we'll pass right through the battle grounds."

"So, you think they're was a skirmish?"

"You heard the gunfire. You know we didn't fire first but if they were so bold as to fire first then they're gone. Alas with their maker."

"I' going to ride out and see what happened. If as you say they fired first we may have wounded."

"Would you like me to ride with you?"

"I'd be honored," Moses said helping Maya onto her horse. Off with a gallop Moses soon caught up with her.

"I see them. Look over the next ridge."

Moses and Maya descended upon the group some were even relaxing in small groups of three or four around open fires. After walking through the camp, Maya finally spotted Elise. A young man tendering her arm.

"What happened? Are you okay?"

"I'm fine ma. Just got nicked."

"It's nothing Miss Maya. It's only a flesh wound," the young man wrapping Elise's arm said.

"Thank you, sir. Do you mind if I take a look at it?" Moses said intervening.

The man stepped aside to allow Moses to take a look.

"What happened, Elise?"

"I'm not exactly sure to tell you the truth. I started to approach the man when he opened fire on me. My men opened fire when they saw I was hit. Cut 'em all down within minutes. He would rather sacrifice his whole clan than kowtow to a niggra. One or two had the good sense to run when the shooting started."

"And why didn't you send someone to let us know what was happening? You had to know we were worried?"

"I should have. But I was waiting for them to come back with reinforcements before heading back. I didn't want to have them follow us back to the train and endanger innocent lives. The way I see it right now those that got away are waking every hilllbilly in these mountains to come and join them. We're just waiting."

"You're probably right but if you're right we may need the entire train to get involved."

"Your call ma."

"Have the wagon train brought up."

"You sure ma? You know there all bedded in for the night."

"I am aware of that, but I don't think having a mile gap between us and the train is a good move. If they get between us, we'll have no contact and be essentially fighting two battles. There's strength in unity," Maya said.

No slouch in the art of war she'd spent many a lonely afternoon in the major's library reading. She remembered the major making such a fuss when he was able to have the French translation of The Art of War by Sun Tzu translated into English. He had seemed so enamored by it that she felt almost compelled to read it whenever she got the chance. How many times had she read it? At least ten or twelve times memorizing whole passages for times such as these.

"Your mother's right," Moses said loud enough so only she could hear as he rewrapped the bandage on her arm.

"I knew you cared," she whispered back smiling as she did so. "We can always sneak away later. You know mother's sleep by nine and I have other things that need tending besides my arm."

Moses ignored her teasing and when he was sure the wound was cleaned and bandaged correctly he turned to Maya.

"I'm going to bring the train up."

"Okay. You be safe Moses," Maya said grabbing his hand and squeezing it tightly

The tall, handsome, thirtyish, man jumped into his saddle and soon made his way over the mountain pass. Riding quickly, he heard noises from the woods around him and only hoped he would have enough time to make it to the train and have them join up with Elise's men.

Riding into the camp at breakneck speed. Moses shouted.

"Pack up! We're moving out! Arm yourselves! There could be trouble!"

Mothers scurried about grabbing the babies and small children while the men grabbed their rifles and gathered their horses. Despite the alarm there appeared to be a quiet order as this were not the first alarm to have gone off with the niggras from the McClowry place. There were always alarms there. There were alarms when the major got upset with Maya at three or four in the morning and had every niggra wench line p for him outside of the big house. Then there were alarms when a runaway was caught and brought back for all to see what happens when you run. And then there were just the general alarms when the major was drunk or had something profound to say. And for the most part this was no different. It was an alarm that said they not the Jews were the persecuted people and this latest alarm just suggested that the persecution was continuous and ongoing.

Fifteen minutes later, all were up, in position and ready to move forward. Killah and Phoenix troops were to ride close to the woods to draw fire if there was any. Moses was sure that there would be.

"Stay right outside of range and if they begin to fire try to draw their fire away from the wagon train."

"If they should leave the cover of the woods and try to engage you just remember that I'll be bringing up the rear. We're going to lag back a bit," Alexis said smiling. You know. We're just going to pull up the rear and provide security."

No sooner had she finished a burst of fire came from the nearby woods.

"Someone ride up front and tell Mr. Jameson to swing the train out far and wide and out of rifle range! Tell him to put some distance between us and those trees!" Moses yelled. "You've got our back Alexis?"

"Fo' sho Moses," the young woman grinned. Moses turned and rode towards the gunfire. The train was moving forward at a good clip while Killah and Phoenix led their troops across an open field cautiously in the face of heavy fire. When the bullets began dancing around their horse's hooves Phoenix yelled.

"Break brothers." And with that command his troops broke right while Killah's troops rode left at a wicked pace drawing a steady fire from the woods. The wagon train was passed the woods, and all was quiet. Phoenix and Killah had done as Moses asked drawing fire away from the train and allowing it to pass unscathed as they faded into the woods on either side of the combatants. From what Moses gathered these men trained by Maya were proficient at their duties but even Moses had to wonder about the plight of Killah and Phoenix once they faded into the wood. It wasn't long before he saw their plan develop and come to fruition. The mountain men seeing that the wagon had passed, and any opposition had been scared off by their blistering fire now advanced on the wagon train from the rear. They must have numbered forty or fifty men easily.

With reckless abandon the men rode hard firing at the Colored men who now knelt in an attempt to form a skirmish line between themselves and the wagon. Outnumbered they put up a valiant defense and I wondered how long they could hold out when Alexis, Killah and Phoenix's soldiers showed up laying down a steady fire that caught the mountain men in the crossfire. There was no retreat now and neither Alexis nor Phoenix showed any mercy now.

"Remember Camp Pillow!" Alexis shouted as she took careful aim. A loud crack followed and then the screams of a young man.

"No quarter! No mercy!" It was what the Confederate soldiers had shouted as they massacred three hundred Colored Union soldiers taken prisoner at Fort Pillow. It was a sad thing to watch these men killing each other for no apparent reason other than somewhere along the way they'd been taught to hate each other. There was no escape for those men although they fought valiantly in the face of the inevitable. For Phoenix and Killah this killing thing did not seem to be something that either had a penchant for but was a necessary part of keeping family and loved ones safe from threats just such as these. Alexis was different though. She was full of a venomous hate for anything white and I could only imagine what she must have suffered at the hands of these foul crackers. If she'd just watched the major's treatment of her mother that in itself would have been enough fuel to stoke the fire. It could have just been the way niggras was treated. Whatever it was her hatred was never more evident than in this battle. Everyone conceded she to be the best marksman on the MClowry place and never was that so obvious as it was tonight as she sat patiently in the cubby hole of an old oak tree and squeezed off round after round of deadly fire. In the end it was said that she was responsible for eleven deaths alone. When it was over and she and Killah went to assess the damage and found several lying writhing in pain it was Alexis who walked up to them and shot them in the head at point blank range, execution style.

"No mercy. No quarter! Killah make sure these bodies are buried. Leave no trace. No one should ever know a battle had taken place here." And then as if nothing had happened she rode up to Moses.

"Don't think they'll be messin' with us again. At least not these fools. Come on. We'd better check on mama."

Moses was especially fond of this girl although he wasn't sure why. She was definitely Maya's daughter and resembled her mother in so many ways, but she was different than her siblings who seemed so much more reserved. But not Alexis. Bright and beautiful she always seemed right on the edge like a ticking, time bomb with a short fuse. She went about her responsibilities with a zeal and a gusto a sort of hatred not known to most of us. And she was especially pleased when it came to killing white folks.

"It bothers you killing those crackers don't it?"

"Killing anyone bothers me."

"You had to kill in the army, didn't you?"

"Yes, it was kill or be killed but doesn't mean I had to like it. I don't believe man has the right to pass judgement and take another man's life no matter what he has done. Only God can pass judgement over his children."

"I suppose you're right and then I realize how awful busy the good Lord is and try to lend him a hand," she said smiling before riding ahead.

Moments later, she was back her eyes on the brink of tears.

"What's wrong child?"

"Maya. I mean mama's been hit."

"Is it bad girl?"

"It doesn't look good Moses."

I found it far worse than even she had described with both her collar bone and shoulder both broken from the ball from an old musket.

My soul cried out for her but I could not let her see my tears and so I did my best aided by Elise and others who had some medical know how to reset the bones. When one of the older ladies offered her laudanum for the pain she refused telling the woman to save it for the babies and the elderly who were really in pain.

And she was right. More and more folks were coming down ill with this and that but mostly it was influenza which quickly turned into pneumonia and all I knew was that if I didn't get this wagon train out of the mountains soon there would be no train. Funerals were a weekly thing now but Maya in a show of fortitude made each and every one with always some kind words to share for the dearly departed.

"How are you doing baby. I could be better I suppose but then who am I to complain? I have you here by my side. What more could I ask for?"

Moses smiled. He believed this woman and why shouldn't he? But she like everyone in the train was relying on him to get them through this latest adversity. Moses threw the saddle on his horse who was quickly being covered with snow. He didn't know how many times it had snowed in the past week, but it didn't look as if it had any intentions of letting up. There was little he could do but he needed to get away to clear his head.

"Where you headed baby?"

"Just going to ride out and see what the lay of the land looks like up ahead."

"Alexis and Elise tell me there's grumbling throughout the camp so I was going to pull everyone together tonight, so they could ease their grievances."

"Trust me sweetie. I know their grievances. This weather makes travel hard and brings on illness. They're tired and want to know when the hell this will all be over. That's their only grievance and we still have another week, week and a half of these conditions unless they want to really push it and then we can be out of the mountains in a week."

"Can I tell them that?"

"Absolutely. Anything that will give them hope."

"Kiss me my lover," Maya said smiling. From what Moses could observe she was healing nicely. It seemed like the farther she was from her North Carolina residence the warmer she became. Her girls said it was the Moses factor but whatever it was Maya accepted her mantle as queen and with Moses was intent on leading her folks from bondage.

"Should be back in no more than an hour. Let Elise know so she doesn't send another rider out," Moses said kissing her on the cheek before turning the big black roan and galloping into the cold, darkness.

Twenty minutes later the camp gathered around to hear what Maya had to say but there were murmurings.

"Tain't like her at all to pick up strays along the road and just take to 'em like that."

"As if she ain't got enough strays of her own."

"Ain't dat da truth. Now we up here in dese mountains followin' this fool and I'll betcha any amount of money that he lost. Say he went out befo' this here to scout around. I think he went out, so he don't have to face us and tell us the truth. He lost."

"I sho' hope not. McClowry's won't the best but Lord knows the weather was tolerable. But this shit..."

"Miss Maya followin' him just like we is. And I guess if she got faith in him then we should too. She ain't never lead us wrong yet."

"That's true but I's just as ready to head back home than go any further. At least I know the devil there."

"I'm going to pretend I didn't hear that ladies. Gather yourselves together! By God!" Maya screamed. "How long have you withstood the atrocities of being owned by some white man. Today we at least have the chance and the opportunity to know real freedom."

"Folks are dying Maya," someone shouted.

"Folks are always dying. It's a part of life. But we can't look back. We must always look forward, so we can move forward. Yes, it's true. Many of us have taken ill but with the good Lord leading us we cannot possibly fail. Sister Mary how old do you reckon you are?"

"Well my first remembrances put me somewhere in my late eighties, early nineties. Can't rightly pinpoint it exactly."

"And has the good Lord taken care and provided for you up until now?"

"Yes, he has."

"So why would he abandon you now? Come on people! Gather yourselves. Moses assures me that we'll be out of the mountains in a week."

"No disrespect Miss Maya, but what do we know of this man Moses?"

"I know that he has made this trip seven times to aid niggras just like you North and to freedom. I also know that if my Moses was a selfish man he could have gone North alone and not had to endure these mountain conditions, but he sacrificed himself to make sure you made it through safely. These mountain happen to be the safest way."

"I guess so," old Ben chuckled. "I'd be damned if I'd follow someone up through these here mountains. Whatever crime they committed I'd have to let 'em go." Old Ben said smiling his grey beard sparkling with the snow.

"Have faith people! Now let's gather around the fires and try to stay warm. There are extra blankets in the supply wagons and remember it's only one more week."

When the meeting was over Maya went to the edge of the wagon train and looked out in the direction Moses had risen. She needed him, wanted him close. She needed to hear his voice and feel his warmth. She needed for him to reassure her that she would be alright just as she had reassured her people. She knew what he'd told her, but she wasn't convinced. She wanted convincing. And as soon as he got back they were going to find somewhere secluded and she was going to be reassured as well. This she knew.

It was well past an hour now and with no sign of Moses Maya began to worry.

"Elise, Moses isn't back yet? He should have been back long ago."

There was no need to say anymore. Within minutes Elise had assembled a team of twenty-five and was ready to ride.

"Heard Moses could be in some trouble," Alexis said as she rode up. "Let's go!"

It was not long before the group saw lights off in the distance. As they got closer there appeared to be a cabin of sorts off to the side of the road. Alexis motioned for the troops to get down and make themselves scarce.

"I'm going to take a few of my guys and see what's going on in that cabin. If you hear gunfire pull the rest of the men up."

"I'm going with you," Maya said.

"What good will you be with one arm in a sling, ma?"

"Never underestimate me chile. Now let's go."

The seven of them made their way up to the cabin quietly. Now on all fours they crept up to the windows. There were four bearded men passing a gallon jug among themselves. What appeared to be the oldest of the mountain men stood in front of the window not allowing Alexis to get a clear sight of the room.

"Can you see?" Maya whispered coming from the far side of the cabin.

"They got him bound to a chair. Looks like they beat him pretty good. I want that one that beat him alive."

"Stay here mama. I'll take care of this."

"You be careful chile."

"Always mama," her nineteen-year-old said before slipping off into the darkness of the night. "Listen people this is the plan. They got Moses. Mama wants the man that beat him taken alive. Do what you like with the rest. I need someone to create a diversion on the far side where mama is. When they come out to see what all the racket's all about take care of them. Meanwhile, I'll be on the cracker in font of Moses. That's the one mama wants. Is everybody ready?"

Shaking their heads in unison Alexis gave the orders.

"Akeem, I want you and Pete to provide the diversion and just remember mama's over there and she's trigger happy so be careful. Make it loud enough so we can hear it. That's when we'll hit the front door. If he has a gun on Moses, then shoot him but don't aim to kill. If, however, it looks like Moses' life is in danger don't hesitate to kill him. Any questions?" When there was no response. "Then let's do this," Alexis said grinning at her troops.

Not knowing who the two men were coming towards her Maya fired off a shot winging Akeem who screamed mightily as the bullet tore through his flesh. Thinking that was the signal Alexis burst into the room catching everyone by surprise except the leader who still held a revolver on Moses.

"Any of you niggas make a move and your boss here is one dead nigga. Now drop your guns. Daniel grab their guns and any other valuables they has."

Maya watched from the corner of the window.

"Akeem are you okay to shoot? Oh baby, I am so sorry. I didn't know who you were."

"I'm okay. What do you need me to do auntie?"

"Go to the side window. Fix one in your sights and let go when you know you have them in your sights and dead to rights."

"I gotcha auntie," the young man replied almost adoringly.

"Pete?"

"I hear you auntie."

Silently they went about their business. A blast sounded and two of the men fell to the floor. When Maya saw the man in front of Moses go to lift his arm. If he had only kept still. Her shotgun hit him full blast in the lower back cutting him in two. The lone man left standing didn't bother to move. Maya rushed in the cabin with but one thing on her mind. Moses. Aside from a black eye and a contusion here and there he seemed fit as a fiddle on a warm summer's night.

He was out cold when Maya slapped him hard across his face awakening him.

"What the heck," Moses said seeing Maya and the gang all there.

"You said you'd be back in an hour," she screamed at him before drawing her hand back to slap him again.

Alexis grabbed her.

"Come on ma. We came here to rescue him not to finish the work of those crackers. Untie him and get him on the back of a buckboard. Take him back to camp along with Akeem and see that they're looked after. May I have a word with you in private mother."

Maya who was now assisting in addressing Akeem's wounds left his side.

"Mama look. Ever since we've been in the mountains we've been attacked. It's like the woods are breeding crackers."

"It does seem that wat way."

"So, why not let me take seventy-five men and ride out front. If we run into any more trouble we can clear a safe way for the wagon train at the same time without any of them being endangered."

"We've been hit from the back, the side and now the front. I don't see how riding out front would make a difference. Those spying on us are hitting us where they think we're most vulnerable. And that's everywhere. So far and thanks to you we're turned them away each time. I think I'd feel better if you'd stay close to the train. If it would make you feel better, you can ride up ten miles and see what you can see. If you do encounter resistance I do not want, you to engage. I don't want you to do anything more than count numbers and report back to us. I'm serious Alexis. I do not want you to engage."

"I hear you mommy," she said before kissing her mother goodbye and making her leave. It then dawned on Maya and she rushed off just as the contingent of troops not going with Alexis but back to camp was pulling out.

"Whoa! Whoa! There's a bed in there. Put Moses in there on the bed. We'll be fine until Alexis gets back or the train gets here. But I don't think he should be moved until he has to be moved."

Soon it was Maya, Moses and a small contingent of men guarding the mountain cabin and Maya had to smile at how well things had turned out in the end.

"Moses, baby. Ain't no time to be sleeping now. Looka here sweetie. We got us our own private bungalow for a few hours."

Moses tried to smile but it hurt everywhere.

"I know you're hurting baby but mommy's hurting too. I'll try to be easy with you. Now drink this. It'll help with the pain," she said handing him a small shot glass full of laudanum. And she was right. The only thing he felt were the warm subtle waves rocking him in and out of consciousness.

Maya was moaning and, on the verge, when she heard the sound of horses. Dressing Moses quickly she fluffed her dress and straightened her hair before going out and standing on the porch as the train pulled up.

Moments later the sound of more horses could be heard.

"Where's Moses?"

"In the bed resting. Why what's wrong Alexis?"

"Does he know there's a whole damn town of rednecks about six or seven miles in front of us.?"

"Yes, Alexis I am quite aware of that. I've never come through with a party this big, but this is the time, at night, when we usually push through. Although like I said, I've never come through with no more than a party of ten I'd say we need to go ahead and push through and see how much distance we can put between us and that town by morning.

In the morning we can set up a perimeter defense and allow these good folks to rest up. Let them get a good four or five hours and then we push again. Only way we can get out of these mountains in a week. In the meantime, let's get started and please try to impress that we want complete and utter silence going through this town. It ain't like we can hide five hundred people, but we don't wanna give 'em any excuse like disturbin' the peace or some crap like that."

"Does that answer your question sweetheart?" Maya said hugging the fiery little Alexis.

"Let's get 'em up and moving. That means you too Mr. Moses. I'll send someone in to help you out to the buckboard."

"I'm fine dear. Don't worry about me. Just send me my horse and get the train moving. Tell everyone to be on guard."

"You sure you're alright baby? Why don't you get in the buckboard and at least rest until morning?"

"If the rest of the camp has to be up and pushing through then I want to be right alongside of them. Besides," he whispered. "that just may be safer than lying down anywhere with you around," Moses said squeezing her playfully.

"Oh no you didn't Mr. Moses."

Moses left a smiling Maya standing and rode up front to take the point.

"You're the last person I expected to see up and in the saddle," Alexis grinned.

"Man said it's safer being on the front lines than being left alone with Maya," Elise laughed.

"Poor man. Here he is running from Maya and he runs into you. I don't know which one of you wanton hussies is worst. At least I can understand mama. She thinks she's in love for the first time in her life but you, you just tryna scratch that little feminine itch of yours."

"Hush Alexis!" Elise whispered.

"Truth hurts doesn't it," Alexis giggled.

"Hush gal. There's someone out there," Moses said touching the girl on her arm. "Can you make him out Elise."

"It's pitch black out here I can't see anything, but I can hear him rustling in the bushes not too far over to the left about nine o'clock."

"Think you can put a bead on him."

"Don't know but I can surely try."

"That's like pot luck. Let me and the boys go flush him out. And don't worry I'll bring him back alive."

"Go on gal," Moses said. "She's got a penchant for danger, doesn't she?" Moses asked Elise.

"No what it is a deep dislike for the white race. When she was around fourteen she tried to stop the major from raping mommy one night. The major was drunk. He beat her and raped her as well. She hasn't been right since. She has an insatiable thirst to wipe them off the face of the earth and is well on her way."

"I didn't know."

"How could you? Ain't like it something she talks about and neither does anyone else. I think everyone's hoping she meets a nice young fella has some children and mellows. It's a reach but either that or she's going to be killed. I think we've all come to accept that. What hurts is that when she's just with us she's beautiful people. She's just terribly hurt and bitter."

"Not only is she hurt and bitter, she's pretty darn good at this whole killing thing. There's a colonel or major somewhere that would love to have her unique skills. But there's little or no need for her skills where we're going so we have to come up with a plan to slow her down." Moses concluded.

"Funny thing I've noticed about you Moses," Elise said the usual smile gone from her face.

"Yeah, what's that Elise?"

"That your name is Moses and here you are leading your people out of bondage but there are others that you can help, and you choose not to."

"I'm not sure I understand," Moses said now totally confused.

"I know that as much as Alexis admires and trusts you—and that's hard for her to do being that you are a man—that you won't take the time or effort to exorcise her from her demons. Don't you see if you would just give her some time and attention she would stop with her obsession for killing. You could do the same for me if you had a mind to."

"That may all be well and good, but I think you should clear this with your mother first before directing this at me. Whatever she says I will agree to." Moses considered his words carefully and thought of Maya's most recent philanthropic endeavors which had her hand him over to her friend Sadie. Then again, it could end up looking like he as asking permission. He wondered why women had to be so difficult. It seemed the older he became the less he knew about women. Now and when he finally thought he'd found his soulmate she too came with baggage in the form of daughters his age who saw nothing wrong with sharing there soon to be stepfather. It was all a bit too much but now was not the time to think about it.

The town proved to be peaceful and quiet. Moses was pleasantly surprised at how well disciplined the train was pulling through. Aside from the occasional whinny of one of the horses there was not a sound. Granted most of the folks were sleeping but that was all part of the plan and why it was smart to leave at night. In the morning they would switch positions and those now sleeping would drive and they would not stop until they were out of the mountains. Passing through without incident everyone breathed a heavy sigh of relief.

Temperatures were warming now, and it was apparent that spring was right around the corner. The Appalachian Mountains of Virginia had taken its toll, but the weather brought a change of mood amongst the camp and for the first time in months there seemed a renewed sense of hope. It had been two days since Moses had been out of the saddle as he rode point for the train. Maya seeing him nodding in the saddle had Killah and Phoenix fill a buckboard with goose feathers and hay before bedding him down.

It was hard to tell how long he'd slept but when he awoke he found the train to be still rolling along at a fairly good clip. This pleased him although he couldn't—for the life of him—figure out how he'd ended up in the back of this buckboard.

"So, you think you could alleviate some of Alexis' problems if you were to have a relationship with her? Funny thing is I believe that would be a viable solution, but you know what?

"Maya."

"Much as I love my daughter she's just gotta work her way through her issues. I ain't sharin' my man with noone. Did that once and still regret I did it. And believe me baby I know who's behind all of this. She wants you too, but she doesn't know how to come about asking me on her own behalf."

"Maya, I want you to know I had absolutely nothing to do with that. Elise propositioned me, and I told her to ask you to get her to leave me be."

"You don't have to tell me Moses. I know my girls. Once they set their eyes on something they want there's not a lot I or anyone else can do about it."

"So, I see. I'll be fine. Listen. We are about two weeks south of D.C. Once we get there we're free. It's a whole new world. You'll see niggras all dressed up in all the latest finery struttin' up and down Pennsylvania Avenue. You'll see niggras in all kinds of professions. Frederick Douglass has a fine home here. Right now, we're approachin' Roanoke. Roanoke is Virginia but it's still the mountains, so we'll still be dealing with these redneck crackers until we get up around D.C. so tell everyone to stay on their guard. I know they're feeling a little better with the weather and now that we're out of the mountains but we're still not out of the woods."

"I gotcha. I'll spread the word for them to tighten up."

"Hope I didn't interrupt anything important," Elise said always smiling. Her smile was infectious and today was no different. "Damn mommy! You think you could spare him for just one night. I'll send him back all in one piece."

"Is there something you wanted gal?" Maya barked at her oldest daughter.

"Testy, aren't we? In any case there are about a hundred men in uniform about five miles up the road. And they're obviously waiting for us."

"Okay. Stop the train. They've been pushing hard for the past couple of weeks. Tell them to pack it in and rest up for the next couple of days. Make sure your snipers as well as the rest of your troops are bedded down and well rested. I'm assuming that's your major trying to come collecting on what he still believes to be his property."

"Yeah, well I can tell him face-to-face that I ain;t nobody's property and I dare that cracker to raise a hand. I'll cut him down right there in front of his men and send their asses packin' to."

"I see it a lil differently. You play chess Maya?"

"No, always wanted to learn though?"

"Same here but we're going to act like this is a chess match. We have plenty of provisions and the weather's nice, so we'll sit and rest up and rehearse a strategy for attacking them until we have it down pat.

Then we'll wait. We'll turn it into a war of attrition. With his depleted bank account which led to your increased account it'll be hard to keep those troops out there on promissory notes that have no worth."

"I see you 've given this some thought."

"Been planning on this for weeks. The more we rest at this juncture and rehearse the stronger we'll be."

"Elise can you take Alexis and give me a detailed scouting report by morning?"

"Alexis is already there," Elise said on her way out the door.

"As for you m'love I'm putting Phoenix and Killah on you at all times. Don't trust the major. Don't know what lengths he'll go to get you, but I know there would be no limits if it were me. Now do me a favor and let the folks know they are to relax. We'll be here for a few days."

The folks were glad to hear the news and were long overdue for a rest. That night the camp roasted a few pigs drank a little home-made hooch and were in good spirits. Maya had other plans and Moses was surprised that he hadn't seen her in hours. Picking up the corn cob pipe he lit it and strolled through the camp speaking to the good folks as he passed. Finding Maya's buckboard, he was surprised to find her with her kids surrounding her. It was the first he'd seen them all assembled at the same time.

Maya seemed to be drawing on a blueprint and referring to a book on something or another.

"What's up lady?"

"Oh, nothing. Just trying to plan for our future," she said not looking up from her sketching.

Seven old Jeremy had become one of Moses favorites and when the little boy saw him he yelled, "Moses!" before running at breakneck speed and jumping in the man's arms. "Moses, I'm going to have my own room in our new house. That's what mommy said. She said we're all going to have our own rooms."

"Is that right?"

"That's what mommy says. Are you going to come and live with us too? Are you going to have your own room too?"

"Right next to mine," Elise grinned. "Now get down and let Mr. Moses be. You're about a worrisome child."

"Elise be nice to your brother. He's seven you know, and he loves Moses. What's wrong with that? Moses is quite capable of shooing him away if he gets on his nerves. What's wrong? Are you jealous?"

"Touche! And you're right. Let me get outta here. It's about time for me to relieve those at the front."

"Come here girl and give your mama a kiss and a hug. I didn't hurt my baby's feelings, did I?"

Elise giggled as Maya nuzzled her oldest daughter's neck.

"You be careful out there, sweetie."

"Always."

"Tell me something. Have you seen any chinks in the armor? Any weaknesses that we can exploit."

"Yeah they have their back to a cliff with no escape route. If we could lay down some heavy sniper fire for a day or two I think we could force them into an out-and-out surrender. They can't retreat. There's nowhere to go. At best all they can do is surrender. We leave them barefooted, weaponless and take their food stores as well as their horses and let them return as best they can under those situations. I don't think we'll have to worry about them again."

"Sounds like a plan to me. Let's start laying down some of that sniper fire now. Send in two teams. It's still enough light left in the day that we can start leaving some hurt on 'em today. Brilliant idea Elise. Yeah, send in two teams and tell them to shoot to maim. Tomorrow we'll keep two teams trained on 'em all day. We're going to potshot them til their nerves are frazzled. If they move to go pee I want a bullet trained on 'em."

"I want a chance at that bastard personally. So, if by any chance he's taken alive I want him. Do y'all understand? I'm laying dibs on him. He's mine."

"Grab your team," Elise barked at her sister. "I'll meet you at the front."

Forty-five minutes later. The two sisters had positioned the twenty-four snipers at integral points with a clear view of the camp in front of them. Positioning them in trees and behind rocks with a clear sight of the troop's camp, Alexis only awaited the command.

She had other plans though. Once under sniper attack she and five of her most trusted lieutenants would sneak into the soldier's camp and kidnap the major. Once in her custody the rest of his troops would head home defeated or, so she hoped.

Giving the command Elise caught the major's troops who were sitting around camp fires sipping coffee and spinning colorful yarns. There arose loud screams and then what amounted to chaos as soldiers dove for cover. And then just like that it was over but as soon as things seemed quiet enough and a soldier would move there would be another scream as he too was winged. There remained a good deal of yelling and screaming in that camp that day as the soldiers remained pinned down for hours as sniper teams were shuttled in and out.

Unable to assemble the soldiers stayed put finding whatever cover they could find. As the night came on and the visibility became less Alexis and her team moved up close enough to see their eyes and kept them pinned down until the morning when the snipers returned. Hungry and thirsty the men were now cut off from their provisions which Alexis gladly confiscated in lieu of her not being able to locate the major. There were hams, greens, yams, sugar, coffee, hard tack and more. In the five wagons that she confiscated there was enough food to easily have fed the wagon train for months.

"A major? I suppose that's one of the reasons that the Rebs lost the war," Moses laughed. "Who would put their troop against a backdrop with no escape route and nowhere near any running water? Who does that Maya?"

"The major would buy the books on strategy and warfare but that was all for looks. I was the one who read 'em. He didn't read any of them. That was all just for show."

"And that's just why he finds himself in the situation he's in today. Pinned against some rock with no food or provisions and no access to water."

"Arrogance in his ignorance is also a major factor. He does not believe a niggra can ever outmaneuver him because niggras are by their very nature inferior."

"We'll see if he still feels that way on his long walk back to North Carolina."

After one full day of sniper fire the major sent out the white flag.

"Didn't take nearly as long as I thought it would. A bunch of weak bastards. Where's Lexis? Figured she'd be yelling 'no mercy, no quarter 'bout through here."

"Well, let's see how he wants to conduct his surrender."

The young rider approached handing Elise a letter.

"This here letter is supposed to go to a Miss Maya," the young man was obviously scared out of his wits and by this time was wondering if he were going to be allowed to leave or be killed right there on the spot. Wild niggas was capable of anything. The major had commented just last night.

"You wait right there young man," Elise barked at the young man. "We will have your answer momentarily," she watched Phoenix take the letter and ride off to his mother.

"What is it?" Maya asked.

"A letter from the major," Phoenix answered.

"Well, don't just stand there. Read it to me."

"He wants to meet face-to-face to discuss returning you and the rest niggras home."

"Do you have a piece of coal. Write this and deliver it. That has never been our home. And no, I have no wish to meet with you. Here, however, is your option. You can choose to abandon whatever it is you are attempting to do and carry your ass on home or you can resist and watch me slaughter every one of your men and leave you alive to know that you're responsible for their deaths. It's your decision."

An hour later the major replied.

"Let it be known that I bought and therefore own the lot of you and if you think you're just going to walk away then you're crazy as hell and everyone that I catch I'm going to beat the hell out of personally."

After reading this, Maya lost it.

"Unleash everything we have. Let's let him feel the wrath of niggra bondage. No mercy! No quarter! But when all is said and done I want the major brought to me alive. Is that understood?"

"Yeah ma," Phoenix answered.

"Call me when you have that bastard in custody," Maya said hugging Phoenix.

Maya continued to work on her sketching. Fourteen bedrooms was a lot and she wondered if she's have enough money to do all the things she wanted to do. A school, a church and a home all seemed necessary but where would she acquire the money? Moses mentioned a lumber yard. Maya's thoughts drifted. She was almost there. Freedom was only a couple of weeks away.

It wasn't until the third day when the major down to only seventeen men decided to throw the towel in and raise the white flag of surrender. The major's troops had fought bravely and inflicted casualties as well with one dying and six of Alexis and Elise's men suffering wounds.

Alexis was so upset at this that when the major finally decided on surrender it was Alexis who rode in and accepted the surrender but not before having the remaining seventeen troops dig their own graves. Once they were finished she had the major sit in front as she summarily walked the line of surviving troops shooting each in the head and watching them fall backwards into their freshly dug graves.

"Mama wants to see you. That's the only reason why you're still alive. If it were up to me I'd have you die a thousand, horrifying, deaths."

"Why Alexis? I've always liked you."

"How can you even say that you bastard? You raped my mother and me in the same room at the same time and you have the nerve to tell me you've always liked me? My God just think at where I'd be if you hadn't liked me. Now git your ass up and come on."

A half an hour later Alexis shoved the major in front of Maya who still sketching never bothered to look up.

"Maya," the major said smiling knowing that she held the keys to his destiny. "Maya please tell me how we let things get to this point? I'm sure we can think of a reasonable solution to all this pain and agony. You have killed all my men. What more can you possibly want? You've taken everything I have."

"I understand major. When I was just a girl you took everything, I had."

"And I had a right to do that, Maya. I owned you. You were my property."

"First of all, you and I know that you can never own one of God's children and second of all you are not are not a dumb man major. You and I both know that there is a higher law. There is God's law and under God's law you know that it is wrong to enslave another human being. And under God's law rape has never been condoned. You however chose to only follow God's law when it condoned your actions. I have agonized under your ownership, but I do not seek retribution for the inhumanity that you have shown towards me and my family. There are however, those that do hold animosity towards you and the treatment of their mother and so I will turn you over to them now major. I wish I could say it was nice to have known you, but I'd be lying. Do you want him Elise?"

"No. I'm like you ma. If I never see this backwards cracker ever again that would suffice. Alexis has plans for him though."

"Then tell her he's all hers. Tell her to take him far enough from the camp that he won't upset the camp with his screams."

"Come on Maya. You can't be serious," the major said incredulously.

"Get him out of my sight."

"What do you want us to do with him?"

"I could care less. How are you feeling about the major's future Elise?"

"I'm like you ma. I could care less what happens to him. I'm sure Alexis has some ideas of what should be done with him."

"I'm sure she does," Maya laughed.

Sending her little brother Jeremy to fetch Alexis Elise had no need to see what transpired and instead rode off to help Moses with the burial detail.

Alexis, finding out the major was hers to dispose of as she saw fit was expedient in her sentence. After a short tribunal made up of her peers and a few of the major's most respected niggras it was decided that he should receive the death penalty. It was Alexis however, that decided that he should be both whipped and castrated. Once sentenced she summoned her brothers, Phoenix and Killah to carry out the sentence. And just like back at the McClowry place everyone came out to see the judgement passed on the major. Only this time no one had to be summoned. Maya could only imagine how this man, this man who'd treated his niggras like chattel, no better than the ox or plow horse he labored with no regard to their welfare felt now as those same niggras applauded every scream that the whip provoked.

When it was over, and his back was bloody Alexis had two of the older women throw salt into his wounds which brought out even more screams before laying him down on the ground to writhe in pain.

Hours later after making her rounds and looking in on her younger brothers and sisters Alexis and Maya returned to the major. The wagon train had made considerable time and was a good ten miles up the road when the two appeared. The major was semi-conscious but came around at the sound of the riders.

Looking up and seeing the mother of his children he pleaded.

"My God Maya, have mercy on me. You can't just leave me by the side of the road like this."

"Mercy. You speak of mercy. Do you remember me begging you not to rape my daughter, your daughter and you laughed. Well, I have had

mercy on you ever since then and can only hope that
God forgives you for some of the atrocities that
you've committed. I pray he does but Alexis here, on
the other hand is not so forgiving. You've scarred her
for life."

"And now it's time I did the same to you."

"What does that mean?" shrieked the major
seeing no remorse in his daughter's eyes.

"I was fourteen. I was just beginning to show
some interest in boys when a man raped me. How do
you think I saw boys after that? And not only did a
man rape me but my own father was the one to carry
out this hideous act. Mama's right. I am and will
always be scarred thanks to you papa. Now you too
will be scarred. Now get up on your feet you
miserable, filthy, piece of white trash," Alexis said
dragging the major from the side of the road into the
woods beside it.

"Take off your pants or do I need to do it for you?" Alexis shouted.

When the major hesitated Alexis hit him with the butt of her gun knocking him to the ground.

"Why you stupid bitch. You raise your hand to a white man. I will have your ass whipped," he shouted.

Alexis was forced to laugh.

"For some reason, I have the feeling that that same arrogance is the same arrogance that has you in the position you're in today. Now major be a good boy and lose your pants," she remarked raising the gun again.

"Okay. Okay. Please Alexis can't we find another way to resolve this."

"I wish I could major, but I've spent the last five or six years thinking about this day," she replied as she took out a good piece of rawhide and tied his hands behind his back. "You're going to wish you'd been hung by the time I finish with you major, but I can guarantee you one thing. You will never stick this in another woman," she said as she pulled out her razor-sharp Bowie knife grabbed the man's exposed genitals and made a one-inch incision in several places causing the colonel to cry out in agony each time she pierced the skin. And the more the major cried out the more Alexis sliced until overcome with pain Alexis left him to bleed out.

"Is he dead? From the screams I can only imagine. I only hope this helps to relieve some of the bitterness that has come to fester within you over the last few years my daughter."

"You and I both mother but you know I've waited so long for this day to come along and now that it is here and gone I feel no relief. I don't feel any justification. I don't feel anything. He went to his grave being a hateful, racist cracker and I did nothing to change his heart or his thoughts. The only one thing I did was bend to his level and lessen myself in the Lord's eyes."

"That you did my child and that is something you will have to live with for the rest of your days," Maya remarked. "Now come on. Let's get out of here before someone attaches us to the body in the woods.

There was nothing left. And as the dim yellow of the sun started to disappear into the distance and the midnight blue starts to appear the thought of the major was now but a distant memory. All thoughts that belonged to the travelers were now of their new home.

Maya was content with drawing up the plans for her new home while Moses occupied himself with the train and coming to better know his new neighbors.

"So, Moses you think we'll run into any more trouble?" the white-haired Mr. Johnson inquired.

"I think the worst is over, but you can never tell. You can never be too careful," Moses replied. He liked the elderly Mr. Johnson and spent many an evening huddled around a fire listening to the wily old gentleman's tales of Africa and slavery.

"White folks ain't all together responsible for our bondage. The 'cause of slavery is what's gonna be the downfall of this here nation though. The 'cause of slavery is greed. Cotton demands labor and we are that labor. But Africans are as much a part of the slave trade as Europeans, so we can't go blaming the white man for all our problems. And the niggra that don't make an attempt to escape his bondage has no one to blame but himself. I know how hard it is to escape the slave catcher but a niggra that don't try is conceding to being another man's slave because he is not resisting and is accepting the terms of his

condition."

"That may be all well and true, but you have

to respect the niggra's will to live. You know you run

and there's a good possibility that you won't run

again."

"I am living testament that you can run and

live to run again. And I do hear you Moses and you

may be right, but the slave has an obligation to fight

the noose around his neck. Use arson and burn the

crops. Burn the whole dam plantation down if

possible. Poison is another alternative, but one

cannot just allow himself to be enslaved without some

type of retribution towards this foul institution."

"I agree. And now that we have our so-called

freedom what do you think our next plan of action

should be?"

"You and I know that freedom ain't nothin' but a word to us niggras. Now that we has got our freedom does that mean I have the right to do anything or go anywhere I want without being harassed and abused? I don't think so. But until we are allowed to participate without being considered second-class citizens then we have no choice but to do what the great Frederick Douglass suggested."

"And that is?"

"Agitate, agitate, agitate," Mr. Johnson said handing Moses a tin cup of homemade hooch. "Try this Moses. This is just a lil' homemade wine I've been sitting on for some time now. Tell me if it's ready?"

"Can't do that right now Mr. Johnson. Got some more rounds to cover before the nights out. If you've got a jar though I'd e glad to take some with me. If it's anything like the last it should help me sleep."

"Thought that was Maya's department," the old man teased.

Three weeks later we reached the outskirts of D.C.

"Lord knows there is a whole mess of Colored folks in this here D.C." Maya remarked grinning broadly. "And these here ain't no common field hands. These is hi-falutin niggras. Looks like they gotta little money."

"The largest and most well-known hotel is owned by a niggra and it's not uncommon for us to own businesses here. Half of the city is Colored. That's a lot of Black folks," Moses said pridefully as if he had some part in the Colored migration to D.C.

Maya grinned broadly exhibiting all of her pearly whites. Moses couldn't remember seeing her happier.

"I wanna thank. You have certainly delivered on your promise," Maya said hugging Moses causing the horses and carriage to swerve into the crowded pedestrian traffic causing a middle-aged white man with his two young daughters to jump out of the way.

"You'd better learn to drive that thang nigga."

Moses gathered the team in and stepped down from the carriage.

"I do apologize sir. The team seems to have gotten away from me."

"If you want to keep that team you'd better get you and your whore away from me now."

"And if you don't want your girls to see their daddy get embarrassed in the middle of Pennsylvania Avenue you'd better apologize to my fiancée this instant. Don't and I'll blow your cracker ass away from here," Moses said smiling so as not to draw any unwanted attention as he unhooked his holster.

Seeing this the man's whole demeanor changed as he glanced his daughters then Maya.

"Sorry ma'am. No disrespect intended," he remarked tipping his hat while gathering his daughters and making his leave.

"I see things ain't a whole lot different. Ain't a whole lot changed. Crackers are still crackers no matter where you go."

"Funny you say that. You know D.C. was the first to free the slaves but you absolutely right and like Mr. Johnson always be sayin' laws don't change mindsets."

"Old as he is ol' man Johnson is still wise beyond his years. That cracker made me angry," Maya said almost apologetically the venom still spewing from her eyes. "You wasn't going to shoot him in the middle of the highway with all them people around."

"In the short time that we've known each other have you ever known me to commit to something and not follow through?"

"No, can't say that I have."

"Alrighty then," he said smiling at his best girl and coaxing the horses to a trot. Maya was once again fascinated by all the colorfully dressed Coloreds who paraded the streets as if they owned them. Pulling up in front of the swanky Wormley Hotel Moses jumped down and handed the reins to the young niggra attendant. Walking around to Maya he lifted his arms to her.

"I know you don't think I'm going in there dressed like this?"

"Ain't no prettier girl in there. Am I right?" Moses said turning to the young man.

"I ain't seen one, suh," the attendant said looking at Maya a grin stretched wide across his face.

"See. And I believe this young man has seen everyone going in. Now come on."

Maya was surprised to find a good many of the patrons looked like her.

"They let Colored folks in here?" Maya whispered.

"No. The question should be do they let white folks in here. This is a black owned establishment."

"Are you serious?"

"Quite. Such notable people as Mr. Douglass and the late President Lincoln have both raved about the food here. The restaurant has been noted for its cuisine."

"And niggras own it?"

"Yes, Maya. You see there are possibilities. I didn't say it would be easy but someone with your know how and creativity should have no problem establishing yourself."

"But why not right here, Moses? Why do we have to go any further?" Maya said walking through the lobby doing her best to take in everything. What she didn't realize was that she was the one attracting attention as every head in the place turned to see who this woman of royalty was. Oblivious Maya continued her tour oohing and ahhing as things caught her fancy.

"My dear, there will be plenty of time to browse the sights, but I brought you here for dinner and I have a little more than five hundred folks under my watch who are in a country they have never been to before. There are all kind of dangers just a waitin' to happen. They are fair game for every robber baron and road thief out there."

"My goodness you are a worrisome ol' hen if I ever saw one. You just remember before they ever had a father they had a mother," Maya said winking at her man. "You know they're in right good hands with my children. Lest you forget I trained them and they are quite capable of taking care of themselves and you if need be. They'll be fine Moses. Stop your worrying and enjoy the night. How long did you say we were in D.C. for?" Maya said leaning into Moses now that she had said her piece. Just helping him to think a little more logically and stay within himself she thought grinning mischievously.

"May I order for you Maya?"

"You certainly may," Maya said still sightseeing from her seat.

After placing their order Moses turned to Maya.

"Sweetheart, I'd like to ask you something."

"Can I tell you something first."

"Sure."

"Well, you know how I'm doing the planning for the house and wanting each of my children to have their own bedroom even if they don't choose to live there they'll always have a place to call home."

"I understand."

"Well thing is I think we may have to add another bedroom."

"What are you saying, Maya?" Moses grinned.

"Are you sayin' what I think you're sayin'?"

"You are going to be a father Moses."

"That's wonderful. Kinda goes along with what I wanted to ask you Maya."

"Oh yeah and what could that be?"

Dropping to one knee in the aisle in plain sight of everyone.

"Will you marry me Miss Maya?"

Everyone in attendance awaited her answer.

"If you don't get up off your knees Moses X," Maya said now embarrassed to no end.

"These good people are waiting for your answer."

"Yes, I'll marry you if you'd just get up off your knees," Maya grinned while everyone in Wormsley's cheered this woman of royal heritage.

Moses would slide the ring on her finger late but for now he was content with showing his queen some of the finer things in life that the South wouldn't allow a niggra.

"So, if I had a hankering to I could rent a room right here in this here Wormley Hotel with the delicious food. How do you call it cuisine? Oh my! I could get used to this. And why was it you said that we can't stay in D.C.?"

Moses laughed out loud and once again all eyes were on the newly engaged couple in the center of the room.

"It has been quite a day for you hasn't it. You should sleep well tonight."

"I will. Right upstairs. I can only imagine what the bed is like. I'm sure they have room service. I read about it. It's where they send the food up to the room. Let's have our food sent up to the room then we can have a romantic dinner on a night so many good things have happened."

Dinner was served in the room and Maya and Moses had their dinner by the fireplace in the bedroom of the suite. Maya was sure she had to scrap her plans for the house after seeing the hotel suite. And the food. It was her first time having lobster and she finished three before Moses convinced her that if she continued she'd end sick from eating such rich foods. And the more she felt her new-found freedom the angrier she became at the whole of the white race.

"I wish all the folks could experience this one time while we're here," Maya mused.

"And what's stopping them?"

"You mean common everyday field niggras is allowed in here too."

"Long as they got the money to afford it. Besides what are we but common everyday field niggras."

"Touché," Maya grinned in embarrassment. "And what was wrong with our making D.C. our final destination m'love? I do believe I asked you this several times. Are you purposely ignoring me?"

"Not at all," Moses laughed grabbing the golden faced Egyptian queen in front of him and kissing her passionately.

"This is just something you have to trust me on. But it gets better as you go North. It gets better."

"I'm trusting you cause I ain't been nowhere and ain't never seen nothin' so if you tell me it gets better than this and you was the one that brought me here then I believe I gots ta trust you. Oh, Moses we gonna have the biggest weddin' when we get wherever it is that we're going."

Moses spent the remainder of the week acting as tour guide for the camp taking groups of twenty-five or thirty, many who had never been off the McClowry place into the city to show them the sights. Most were like Maya and wanted to know why they had to go any further. D.C. even with its pitfall was good enough for them. It took a good strong emotional speech from the queen herself to get her trusty congregation to continue having faith in the man who had delivered them thus far. Funny thing was Maya had truly bought into Moses way of thinking and after hitting every colored seamstress and clothier in D.C. Maya had grown quite a collection of the finest finery to be found. For many she already had the designs in her head and only had to have them put on paper and then in her favorite fabric. Maya paid handsomely to keep them all up and working twenty-four seven, so they'd be ready when she pulled out. But after dining out and seeing the best of what D.C. had to offer Maya was more than content to stay with the camp on **the** outskirts of D.C. pestering Moses when he wasn't giving some group a tour of D.C. If she wasn't getting under Moses skin she was playing with her own brood or designing her soon home to be. Oh, and trying to learn the lumber business from Moses and the few books in the major's library that she'd been able to put her hands on.

When Moses finished his days as trail guide and tour director he too was content to sit down, pull out his corncob pipe, (a habit he had only recently picked up from the wily, old, Mr. Johnson), and sit out and just enjoy the warmer, weather.

"I have never seen such a younger older man," Elise commented one evening as she sat down around Moses' fire. She too had a pipe and was content to join Moses in a fireside smoke. "By the way congratulations on the news. I'm happy for you both," Elise said her sincerity obvious.

"How dothe rest of the kids feel about it?"

"You should know lil Jeremy's not the only one who really thinks God sent you to lead them to the chosen land. I think Alexis, Phoenix and Killah are like me and are just happy to see mama happy."

"Well, that's a relief."

"She also told me of your plans to open a lumber yard outside of Boston and supply the ports and boat yards. And I couldn't help but thinking that

a lumberyard requires a good many men to run it.
And as a wedding present I'd like to help you supply
it with manpower."

"And how do you propose to do that?"

"Bring your bedroll and follow me," Elise said
grinning broadly at a shocked Moses. "Come on
Moses. It'll be our little secret. Just a few feel-good
moments is all I'm asking."

"Someone's going to come along and sweep
you off your feet just the way your mother swept me
off my feet. You just have to be patient, Elise."

"Patience don't matter if my sights are set on
you."

"But they no longer are, and I won't hear of
this talk anymore. White folks may not respect our
relationships, but we will have respect among
ourselves and if this man admits to wanting to marry
the woman carrying his child then you as my

daughter should respect that. Now I want no more of this talk. Do you hear me Elise? Nott even playfully. I want this to end now."

"Yes mother," Elise replied clearly embarrassed that she'd been caught red-handed propositioning Moses.

Elise dropped her head.

"I'm sorry mother. It won't happen again. I promise you," Elie said standing and knocking the ashes from her pipe. Moses thought he saw a tear stream don Elise's cheek as she gathered her horse and left.

"I'm so sorry baby. But it won't happen again. She's a good girl and I can't really blame her. She had her sights on you from the very beginning," Maya acknowledged.

"She did but that doesn't necessarily mean the feelings were mutual. While she was looking at me I was looking elsewhere, and I can't nor should you apologize for feeling as we do for each other."

"You're right. There's enough hurt out here and believe me my children have suffered their fair share. But I want to be the last person to administer some hurt to them and that's what I'm doin' in this child's case."

"Believe it or not sometimes administering hurt is all a necessary part of life. Young folks are if nothing else adaptive and she'll be fine. I have a feeling as attractive and personable as Elise is she won't be in Boston very long before she brings Thurman or Jackson to meet you."

"You think?"

"I must admit she did catch my eye before I had the good fortune to lay eyes on you."

Maya smiled but dot reply. She'd made the mistake of having him sleep with Sadie when they'd just met but little had changed if she'd ask he would comply. He loved her just that much. But no, that had only created more problems and Lord knows there could and would be no problems especially among family. No, as Moses said she would just have to man up and move on. He'd made it quite clear to both mother and daughter that there was to be no compromise in Elise's case.

Elise wasn't the only concern Moses and Maya had. A blossoming issue among the camp surrounded the overall condition of the travelers who by now were physically exhausted from the four-month journey. The mountains as well as the frequent skirmishes had taken its toll on a people already beaten and broken.

"Moses, can I have a word witcha if you not busy," the man known as Jackson said riding up next to him.

"What's on your mind Jackson?" Jackson and Moses were about the same age and come to be close and rather good friends since their initial meeting and it was nothing for Jackson to sneak away from his wife and kids to share a sip of homemade hooch and pick Moses brain on what it was like to be free.

"Tell me Moses. And you know I ain't one to criticize you on your decisions. I always been loyal to ya but I need to know some things just for my own curiosity."

"I'm listening."

"A lot of us ain't never been off the McClowry place so we ignorant as to the ways of the world. But I'll tell you Washington D.C. was like heaven for most of us. We seen free Coloreds that was dressed just as fine as any white folk and they seemed like they were in control of their own destinies. That's what it seemed like. They owned fine businesses. Now you're telling us that there is a place that's even better for a nigga I mean a niggra."

"Washington is the nation's capital Jackson so you're going to see a lot of pomp and circumstance."

"Not quite sure I know what that is," Jackson said looking a bit puzzled.

"Pomp and circumstance ain't nothin' but niggras lookin' for a place to get dressed up for and D.C. is full of balls and ceremonies that give niggras a chance to show off. But when they wake up in the morning they still cleaning Miss Anne's kitchen. They pretending that they are a part of the whole Washington D.C. social thang and to an extent they are. I ain't takin' nothin' away from 'em but what we don't see is how hard Colored folks have it here. You saw the slave pens. They're still rounding up niggras and sending them back south. Washington D.C. is the dividing line between the North and the South and there are still too many folks that are still fighting the

Civil War. No. D.C. is not the place for a free niggra trying to set roots down and grow his own. I do believe that both Philadelphia and Boston present more opportunities for us Coloreds as a whole."

"You would know better than me so lead the way my brother. Tell you what though. There was some fine fillies in D.C."

"Aren't you married Jackson?"

"Marriage ain't blinded me man. Oh, my fault. I forgot you're still in the honeymoon phase and all you can see is Maya," Jackson said laughing.

"I ain't blind. I just ain't never seen anything that even closely compares to what I already have."

"I can't really argue with you there. Miss Maya is one helluva catch," Jackson said smiling at his friend. "Let me get outta here before the missus puts the hounds on me," Jackson said wheeling his horse around and heading for his wagon.

Moses continued to pull slowly on the pipe before tapping the ashes out and refilling it. He understood the folks and their way of thinking. Sure, D.C. appeared to be the promised land but that was only because they knew of nothing else but he Moses X would show them that there was more and teaching them to never settle.

"Evening Moses. You seen ma?" Killah asked.

"Not lately, but if I were a betting man I'd bet that she's at the back of the wagon working on the plans for her new house."

"She tells me she may have to add an extra room on."

"Same thing I'm hearing," Moses said as he stirred the ashes of the fire until flames shot up angrily in response to being disturbed.

"Are you ready for it?"

"Haven't had much time to think about it. I've been so preoccupied with trying to get the train through with no major incident and no casualties that I haven't really had a chance to think about it."

"I guess not. To tell you the truth I don't envy you. For you a stranger to take on mama and this whole outfit you have to have a little grit about you. Mama is a handful by herself," Killah said fishing trying to get to know this man better.

"It's all a matter of perspective, how you see things, my good man. I never see things as being hard or out of reach but only as a challenge and I never take on a challenge that I can't win. Your mother is a delight to be around and if I never opened my mouth and just listened I could absorb a wealth of knowledge and I look at this train as family and together we will go to Massachusetts and carve out some land and when we are finished carving out some land we will begin carving out a name for ourselves.

That's the way I see it. Both your mother and these good folks have already enriched my life. The best I can d is try to give something back."

"So, you are serious about taking on this woman with fourteen, soon to be fifteen children? And this is just not a ruse to take an older spinsters money?" Killah grinned knowing he'd shaken Moses with his last sentence.

Doing his best to keep his composure Moses turned to the man five years his junior.

"I am saddened that you would even think to ask me something like that. I don't know you, but I thought I knew you better than that. No. My aim is not money. I am fixed rather well in that area, but it is obvious that you don't know your mother as well as you think you do. If you did you'd know that she is a wealth of knowledge and money pales in comparison to what she has to offer. And if I am guilty of anything when it comes to her it's that I want to drain her of all that she has to offer in the way of knowledge. And it will be my honor if she has me."

"I was only teasing my brother. You mustn't always wear your feelings so close to your heart. You're a good man Moses. Still, I think you underestimate mother. She can be demanding. When she gets that way and you're at your wits end, and ready to walk out I want you to come and get me and together we can work it out. I think we both want the same thing for her. Happiness. But that's not to say that she can't and won't test your limits."

"If I'm correct that's what women do," Moses chuckled. "But I want to thank you for that my brother," Moses said standing and hugging the bigger, taller, man.

"She's a good woman Moses. She deserves better than what she's had."

"And it is my intention that she receives everything she has coming to her."

"Just remember I'm here if you need my help and you will need my help, Moses," Killah said smiling sheepishly before saying goodnight. Seeing he wasn't going to get any peace of mind here Moses put his pipe away and decided to head in. It had been another long and grueling day. Was there any other type nowadays? But first he would stop and say goodnight to Maya as had been there tradition since they'd begun this journey. And just as he'd told Killah. She was at the back of the buckboard pouring over her sketches. Coming up from behind he was surprised to find her not pouring over designs for the new house but over dresses she'd designed in her head over the years.

"Hey hon. Was flirting with the idea of starting a small boutique in one of Boston's wealthier, mo' upscale neighborhoods. Throw in some of the latest pieces out of London, Paris and New York and sprinkle a few of my own in with just a name on it. 'Designed by Maya.' Maya will forever be an enigma and that will only draw to the mystique."

"I hear you sweetheart," Moses remarked. Today she was a fashion designer. Would wonders never cease when it came to this woman. One day she was an architect intent on designing her own home with little or no help from anyone. The next day she was designing dresses for an upscale Boston clientele. Tomorrow she could be training the troops for an upcoming battle or raid before mapping out a strategy that would make Hannibal envious. You just couldn't tell but it's what kept things new and interesting and he loved her for both her spontaneity and creativeness.

"Just wanted to say good night before I headed in," Moses said before grabbing her by the shoulders and kissing her lightly on the cheek.

"I haven't seen or talked to you all day and all you have to say when you do see me is good night?"

Moses thought of the conversation he'd just had with Killah and was forced to smile. The young man had just warned him about his mother. Yes. She could be a handful when she had a notion to be.

"I'm tired Maya. I'm going to bed. Have a pleasant night," Moses said.

"Leave me like this no and I'll be forced to come see you when you're asleep and most vulnerable," she laughed.

Moses knew she was dead serious and hoped to at least get a couple of hours of sleep in before she intruded.

The next morning at the crack of dawn he was up and, in the saddle, when Alexis came riding in hard.

"Moses. Some men said they were part of some sheriff's department came as soon as we got off our posts. Sentries took our places and we made a small fire and made ourselves some coffee when they rode in guns drawn demanding that we show them some papers."

"What kind of papers were they looking for?"

"They weren't lookin' for anything except an excuse to throw shackles on us and ship us back down south. It's all a part of the new Black Codes that give them the right to lock us up or sell us back into bondage if we commit an infraction like loitering. It's just another way of keeping slavery operative."

"The Black Codes huh?" Moses chuckled. "Where did they grab them at and how long ago?"

"No more than five minutes ago and no more than a quarter of a mile up the road."

"How may are there?"

"Two maybe three. I didn't really get a good look at them. I was in the bushes handling my business."

"You have your rifle with you?"

"You already know."

"Alright what I need for you to do is ride up ahead of them. Find a high bluff where you can look down on them. Then I want you to pick off as many as you can. I'll come in behind them and finish cleaning up."

"I gotcha."

A half an hour later Alexis sat high atop a bluff just outside of a small, rural town in southwestern Pennsylvania. Looking down the front sight she had the leader. Come on now. Squeeze gently. Don't pull or jerk. Squeeze gently. Come on girl. This fool has your brother. Before the man's body had a chance to hit the ground Alexis had the

second man in her sights. Still, trying to figure out
what had hit there leader the man was urging his
horse over to his friend's lifeless body when he came
to meet the same end with a crashing thud. The third
of the three highway men didn't bother to wait riding
off when he saw his friends fall from their horses, but
his fate was no different as Alexis drew a bead on
him riding away knocking him from his saddle.

Moses was in the midst of the men now
unshackling them and leading them to their horses.

"Don't know why I even bothered to tell you
anything," Moses teased 'Lexis. "You had the whole
thing under control," Moses said smiling at Alexis.
She was embarrassed standing there now. Almost
shy but beneath this cute, shy exterior loomed a
deadly killer proficient at her craft.

Moses could only imagine how the major had
met his untimely demise. And once this got out it
would only help promote the now growing legend of

Alexis prowess in the killing game. This wasn't good, but on the other hand the people felt more secure having the little lady around and aside from this she was one of the most helpful neighbors always lending a helping hand to those in need. And though every parent knows not to show favoritism among one's children it was clear that Maya favored this child. Perhaps it was because she was the one most damaged and therefore required the most attention. Perhaps it was because she was the one that most resembled Maya in looks and temperament. One may never know but it was Alexis who most resembled her in so many ways that would cause Maya her most pain.

A week and a half later the train rolled to the outskirts of Philadelphia where they set up camp. That first night Moses didn't know how many times he told folks to 'stay together and be careful' as they headed in to see the city of brotherly love. And after speaking to the natives at the local watering holes about life in the city Colored folks they agreed almost to a man that this place with all of its racial problems was still a whole lot better than Washington D.C. with its fine niggras in their fancy clothes.

Here, in Philadelphia, there were people, common folks just like them, working hard, striving carving out a niche for themselves and their families. Philadelphia was no utopia. Not by any means. Colored folks fought every day for their rights but at least here they felt that they had a fighting chance and could effect change in some way. This was good enough for many of the weary travelers on this train and yet Maya was called upon once more to rally the troops.

"Look y'all! We too close. We too close to where we wanna be for y'all to start talking about splittin' up now. We family and we ain't gonna let nothin' tear us apart when we so close. In two weeks, we'll be in Boston building our homes from the lumber we chop which will in turn give us employment and make us self-sufficient. Can Philadelphia guarantee you a job? Well, I can. Now let's get it together. Pack your wagons. We're moving out in the morning."

"What's wrong baby. I didn't feel the usual passion tonight."

"You brought these simple niggas all the way from North Carolina to a land they knew nothing about. You led them and now that we are almost there they have decided that they can now think for theyselves and make smart decisions on something of which they know nothing. I could care less if they come or not at this point. I am sure we can find labor in Massachusetts."

Moses smiled at the feistiness of his woman. She like everyone was exhausted and had little patience.

"You know I spent my entire life worrying about the welfare of these same folks because they was in many cases too damn ignorant to take care of theyselves. And now that they got a little taste of freedom they think that enables them to think when they've never thought before. You know who did the thinking and decision making for them? I did. Now out here in a world they know nothing of they want to make their own decisions. I understand that. But first they must learn to think and make decisions wisely. Your choices end up deciding who you are as a person. But first you must learn to think," Maya spewed angrily.

"I think you're making far too much of it sweetie. Ol' as Mr. Johnson is you still consider him one of your children. You remind me of the major in that sense. These people have always been free. Whether they recognize it or not has always been their choice. When you did the thinking for them and kept things profitable for all involved things were fine. Now they have the opportunity to strike out on their own and who can blame them for thinking that they can now prosper on their own. They are capable. You taught them well but if you think of them as your children then it's time to cut the apron strings. They are like sparrows who leave the nest when they are able to fly. Let them fly Maya. Even if they fail. Let them fly," Moses said letting his emotions get the best of him.

Maya stood there staring at him before breaking into a broad grin.

"I don't think I've ever heard you say that much at one time," she said wrapping her arms around him and hugging him tightly and burying her head in his shoulder.

Moses felt her shoulders and from the sounds he knew she was sobbing softly. Had he caused this? He only hoped not.

"You okay sweetie?"

"I love you Moses X. You know I've never been in love before. Isn't that something? Old as I am I've never been in love before. But I am so thankful that the good Lord has allowed me to finally experience it. Do you know that I've never had anyone who I could confide in. It was always someone coming to me with their problems, but I never had an outlet for mine. I appreciate what you said. I appreciate the fact that you feel strong enough to put me in my place. It's kind of sexy don't you think?"

"A cat with three legs is sexy to you Maya," Moses laughed.

"Oh, come on sweetie you know it's you that turns me on. Come on. It's early. Let's find us a nice quiet boarding house for the night."

"Or we could just find us a nice quiet, place right here under the stars."

"Fetch me the palomino and I'll meet you by the old oak tree about a quarter mile up the road," Maya said turning and putting the finishing touches on her sketch.

"Good chance we're going to run into Alexis and her scouting party up the road."

"We'll just have to deal with that when we get to it."

"By the way, there's someone I want you to meet tomorrow."

"Friend of yours?"

"I would like to think so. I just think you two are of like minds and would appreciate each other greatly."

"His grandfather started the first Colored church here in Philadelphia after being made to sit in the back at the white Methodist church. Broke off

and established the first African Methodist church.

Anyway, his grandson and I went to school together.

He's a leader here in championing our rights. Talk

about a fighter. You'll love him."

"I look forward to meeting him. But no more

talk of fighting tonight. Let's only think of loving

each other. Now go. I'll be there," she said pushing

Moses away. It was warm enough to go down to the

stream and bathe and was surprised to find it empty.

This wasn't the first time he'd opted to take a quick

bath but there had always been someone there.

Tonight, was different and knowing Maya it would be

a good hour before he'd see her. She had to check on

the kids and freshen up herself. To Moses' surprise

the water was warmer than he expected as he slid

down into it. Closing his eyes, it felt good to drift off

thoughtless with no worries. Moments later he

opened his eyes to the soft caressing touch of Maya's

hand as they massaged his back. Damn. It felt good. She was reaching for his genitalia now. On the verge of erupting Moses turned to the woman only to find the young Alexis.

"Alexis! No! Alexis!"

Moses screams drew Maya's attention and no sooner than he screamed did she appear.

"Oh, hell no. I just went through this with your sister. I know damn well I taught you better than this or perhaps I didn't but if you don't get the hell out of that water I'm gonna beat the black off you gal."

Alexis was out of the water in less than a heartbeat grabbing her clothes and never stopping to acknowledge her mother.

"Damn Moses what is it that you have? There's something you're not telling me when I have to chase my own daughters away from you. My girls have always shown me respect—well—that was until you happened along. That's two in one night. But then I'm no different. If I think about you then I want you," Maya said slowly lifting her petticoats as she entered the water.

"Come here darling."

"Maya I'd like for you to meet one of my oldest and dearest friends Mr. Richard Allen III. Richard this is my fiancée the lovely Maya."

"Your story is well-known here in the North. We championed you when they said we were an inferior race. We wrote and spoke of this Colored woman who was responsible for running the most successful plantation in North Carolina while the great Major McClowry was off to keep this inferior race enslaved. The fact that this Colored woman also was the mother of fourteen of his children did not help the slaveowners argument about an inferior race. It is hard to imagine that a man such as the great Major McClowry would entrust his entire fortune and father fourteen children by a member of an inferior race. It's just hard to conceive."

"The late," Maya whispered.

"Excuse me ma'am but I didn't quite hear you."

"I said the late Major McClowry. Maor McClowry met with a rather untimely death in his own private war to keep those once enslaved by him enslaved after they had achieved their freedom. He lost that war too."

"And many more will die before we achieve complete equality in this white man's America. It's a shame but I am sure Boston will fare far better than North Carolina for you and yours."

"That's what Moses keeps trying to convince me."

"Trust me it is far better than here. It will at least afford you the opportunity to be successful and that's all we can ask. The opportunity."

"Listen, Richard we've been here far too long. I just wanted you to meet Maya, but we've got a wagon train waiting on us. We're gonna see you at the wedding though," Moses said hugging his old friend.

Riding away Maya was quiet.

"Interesting fellow. I like him. He's what you might call insightful. He's a thinker."

"I thought you'd like him. And like I was telling Richard we'll see him in a couple of months at the wedding. We may see him even sooner. I may need his power and influence to get this lumber yard up and running with some haste," Moses remarked as he gathered the cinch on the chestnut.

"You fail to forget that I am the common denominator when it comes to us getting up and established."

"How so m'love?"

"I have the money and money is always the common denominator," Maya said her confidence growing. "In fact, right prior to the major's untimely demise I sent for the remaining hundred thousand in the major's savings that he allocated to his children's trust fund."

Moses had to smile.

"Money's always a good thing to have but money doesn't always work in Boston. These people in Boston are a little bit more sophisticated than that."

"I haven't met the man that'll turn down a dollar."

"And you've never been to Boston either. Everyone we contact will have some knowledge or affiliation in the lumber business and no matter how much money you throw at them they're going to look at their own situation first and how our lumber business will affect their own."

"So, what you're really saying is our progress will be determined by others."

"In the beginning, I suppose and at least until we establish a name for ourselves."

The two led the train up the east coast and though all had somehow come from the picturesque coastal state of Carolina none had ever seen the beach or ocean front until now. After two weeks of travel they reached the beautiful beaches of Rhode Island and again the train halted and while there was much discussion among the travelers of continuing the journey. Others considered setting up shop right there.

Maya understood and was in fact quite enamored by the idea of living close to if not on the beach herself. Mr. Johnson as he recalled the last time he'd been on a beach it was when the slavers had loaded him on board ship to bring him here. I'd felt the same way when I first saw the beach some years back but what they failed to understand was that Boston had beaches too.

"What the hell you niggas gonna do on the beach? How y'all gonna feed yo'self? How y'all gonna feed yo' families? Oh, I guess y'all gonna be fisherman now when y'all don't know the goddamn difference between a red herring and a lobster. Now get yo country asses up into those wagons and let's get ready to pull out."

The journey had been long and tumultuous with Maya having to cajole and motivate them to keep on pushing but everyone knew that there was a limit to even Maya's patience and she'd reached her limit way back when they were in the mountains. She'd taken the time to explain it to them on separate occasions and felt no need to explain it again when they were so close. And just like that they climbed up in their wagons and waited for the signal to proceed. I imagine I knew how many of them felt. After all of this riding my legs felt like those of a new born colt weak and gimpy. Yet, on we rode. We were only two days ride from Boston now, so I dug down, deep and tried to stay upbeat and positive. Truth was I was no different than the lot of them. The trail had damn near broken me, so I knew how they felt but here it was me leading them into the vast unknown that was to be there future and now I saw how much of my dreams I placed on them as well. Maya followed suit out of her love for me, but the rest were only following her lead. I only hoped I was doing them right.

They were all equally as pleased of what they saw of Boston and many were quickly caught up in the quaintness and old world feel that is Boston, but their mood changed once they were back in the open fields outside of Boston.

Miles and miles of open fields stood before them and it was some time before they reached a densely wooded area. Now as the dim yellow started to fade off into the distance and the midnight blue begins to appear there also appears a magnificence in the middle of that magnanimous forest. It was all so beautiful, so scenic, so idyllic and what's more this was their new home.

"Call it what you may brothers and sisters. Me. Well the only person I'm calling right about now is the Good Lord Jesus Christ to thank Him for delivering us to our new home. What do you think of the name New Eden?"

There was a loud roar and Moses was almost ashamed of doubting himself. Almost to a person they came to he and Maya thanking them for a safe journey out of that den of hell. Many of the women brought him something they had baked or made for just this occasion while others simply hugged him before shedding a tear.

"Don't thank me yet," Moses laughed. "In the morning the real work begins. We only have a few months before the winter sets in and we're going to need both housing and a lumberyard started. The real work has only yet to begin."

There were no groans, no sighs just gleeful faces with a sense of hope and purpose for the first time in their lives. They were finally free. There were no misconceptions or naive perceptions. They knew it wouldn't be easy but when had it been. At least they would be working on their own behalf.

The next morning the sun rose and the view from high atop the bluff overlooking Boston was nothing short of breathtaking. The dark, threatening clouds that loomed off in the distance could do little to dissuade the niggra travelers. They were ready and quickly divided themselves according to trade.

Moses was surprised at how well the camp was organized. There were blacksmiths and shoemakers as well as well as bakers and woodsmen. Maya had left no stone unturned but what he needed more than anything at this point and moving forward was as many able-bodied men as he could get to knock down some trees. In a day or two and as soon as the paperwork was finalized Maya would own all the timberland for as far as the eye could see.

Eager to get started Moses employed a hundred and seventy-five men who labored tirelessly from the break of dawn until midday without breaking. There were those woodsman who felled trees with surprising speed and efficiency. Once the trees were down there were men who with teams of plow horses loaded the downed trees and delivered them to a most competent team of carpenters who trimmed the wood into the specifications for homes. While still others with a proficiency in masonry and brick laying were already laying the foundations and chimneys for the homes. Moses and Maya left at noon to sign the papers for the land and on their return hours later they found that all were still hard at work. When it was announced that this was now their land a cheer went up to the heavens letting all know that they had truly found their Garden of Eden.

It didn't take Maya long to learn the lumber business and in no time at all the M&M Lumber Company was showing a considerable profit. Maya had a knack for business and proved even more cutthroat than her competitors often undercutting their

bids in an attempt to win every lumber contract.

"Sit down baby. Here let me get you a chair.

Maya, I know you have a fear of losing, of not being

top dog and I'm not sure exactly what it is that drives

you baby. And don't get me wrong that's one of the

things that I love about you. But you have to realize

that these are our neighbors not our enemies. You

have to begin to look at them as more than just being

white folks. We are not at war with them."

"So, what is it that you're trying to tell me

Moses? That I shouldn't put my best foot forward

and use all my God given skills to do the best I can to

provide for my people?"

"Not sayin' that at all and you know it. What

I'm sayin' is be cognizant of others around you. You

don't want to hurt anybody in your quest for

greatness and superiority. When it comes to the point

where people are being hurt and can no longer feed

their families because you put them out of work then
we need to reassess where we are and how we got
here. A man profited off our misfortune once too you
know."

"And now he is subject to his retribution."

"And he may be but that is not for us to
decide. But to impart hardship on another has never
been the Good Lord's way and is not in your nature
Maya."

"And what is it that you propose that I do?"

"You may wanna start by not bidding on
every contract that comes across the table. Let's
concentrate and focus on what we already have. We
don't need to monopolize the lumber business.
There's enough business where we should all be able
to live comfortably for many years to come."

"I'll concede but you know I'm going after the
docks. That's the want I want. We won't ever have

to worry about anything if we get that one. Now come over here and give me a hug you beautiful brown skinned man you."

"I would if I could get my arms around you. You're damn near big as Bessy the cow. When are you gonna let me see my son?" Moses laughed grabbing and hugging her as he rubbed her stomach affectionately.

"Moses! Are you saying that I'm getting fat?" Maya said glaring at him.

"Fat would be an understatement," Moses said laughing before falling backwards onto the bed.

"Well, will just see how many fat women can make her man beg while creating an empire in her spare time," Maya replied while taking the liberty of straddling Moses who was still doubled up in laughter.

"You know the planters say they're going to come in with the best harvest ever and they've had some pretty good one's in the past."

"The motivations different. They're working for themselves."

"Exactly but hear me out. I'm just speculating but what if they do come in with a bumper crop. Why don't we take the surplus and open a lil produce store right in the center of downtown Boston. People would stop on the way home and pick up produce and we could also serve hot food, so they wouldn't even have to prepare anything after a long day at work. Couple that with a bakery. What are you thinking?"

"I'm thinking that this woman of mine is full of surprises and is quite sincere about creating this empire she has imagined for herself," Moses remarked his smile broadening.

"I truly believe that it is a sin if a person doesn't use the blessings that he has bestowed upon them. I'm simply attempting to recognize and utilize every ounce of potential he has given me."

"I understand you. What I don't understand is where you get the drive from."

"I'm not sure either. Sometimes I wonder if it's a blessing or a curse. My mind is constantly going, racing, thinking, contemplating my next move. There are times when I love that aspect of it. There is so much to do and so little time. At other times it can become overwhelming and that's when I turn to you to slow me down and enter some logical reason. It is after all a fact that men are more logical whereas we women are more emotional. Together we create a rather unique balance wouldn't you say."

"None tougher or more formidable," Moses said the grin now gone. "Without hurting others in the process."

"I understand my husband. Now come here and love me the way I need to be loved."

As ordered Moses loved the mother of his child just the way she sought to be loved until the night disappeared with the darkness.

A month later the house that Maya had designed was complete and would rival any southern manor with its marble pillars and veranda overlooking the road coming into the manor. Oh, it was a sight alright and was not viewed in a bad way by any of the residents of New Eden. This was the queens domain and she had earned it taking care of and providing for them all over the years. She not only warranted it, but she deserved it. Anyone that disagreed as subject to a long tongue lashing or worse depending on who you ran into from the tiny, village of New Eden.

Be at a loss

The economic climate in Boston changed rapidly after the war and with the threat of Blacks migrating North seeking jobs at cheaper labor costs the Industrial North began downsizing accordingly.

The Irish never a big fan of the niggras outside of slavery and an outspoken foe of the abolitionist were proponents of the pro-slavery South for just these reasons. They feared more than any other that they would be affected first.

Meanwhile, in a small Irish tavern on the Irish south side of Boston a gang of ordinary street toughs huddled around pints of ale cursing their fate.

"Say Murph you work today?"

"No, went down to the foundry and it as quiet as a church on a Saturday night. I'm telling you it was shut down tighter than my wife's twat. Ain't nobody working mate."

"Been like that ever since them niggas opened that lumberyard just outside of town."

"The problem is ain't none of you been up to welcome our new neighbor's to Boston."

"I got just the housewarming gift for them niggas too," replied the man with the long red beard placing his hand on his gun.

"They say a nigga wench runs the whole thang. Say she a right, pretty, wench, too. They say she brought a bunch of slaves with her from below the Mason Dixon. From what I understand they used to workin' for slave wages. They ain't used to workin' for nothin' so they basically work for free."

"You say she got 'em working for damn near free?"

"Yes, and that' how she's able to undercut everyone's bid. She ain't gotta pay for the damn labor."

Little did they know that Maya paid her folks better than the going rate and had set up her own type of profit sharing among her workers.

"I heared all this talk about her house so me and my boy rode up to see it and I'm telling you it's bigger than the mayor's home."

"Niggas getting' a might too uppity if you ask me. Sportin' like good white folks and stealin' our jobs at the same time. I say we take what's ours back," an older gentleman said raising his glass.

All in attendance cheered.

"Marty you take Jack and Billy and hit all the local pubs and you tell them we're getting ready to put them niggas in their place once and for all.

Less than an hour later the streets in Charlestown were brimming with drunken gangs out to teach them upstart niggas a lesson. In all there must have been close to a hundred drunken men but when it came time to ride only fifty or sixty took to their mounts in front of O'Henry's Tavern. An hour later riding with open flasks these men screaming obscenities of the worst sort stormed up the road to New Eden. It was clear from their tone and banter that a lynching was in the making. It was Elise returning from Boston on a shopping spree who heard the drunken Irish men's boastings on the road. Making a beeline through the woods she knew she would save close to a mile on them this way and hopefully that would give New Eden enough time to gather up arms if they hadn't already. Elise rode the spotted chestnut with all the haste and speed she could muster. Seeing the sentries at the front gate Elise jumped down from the horse.

"Get everyone up! Tell them to arm themselves and hurry dammit!" Elise yelled at the two sentries. "They're about a mile out. Have them put guards around the lumber yard and mill."

Minutes later the men of New Eden had formed a perimeter like a seasoned army battalion, men filling in the gaps as they arrived.

"Moses. Mommy. Did you get the word?"

"How could we help not get it with all your screaming and yelling, sweetie?" Maya teased as she strapped on her 45 caliber pistol and grabbed her rifle.

"Ignore her Elise. Are the sentries posted? Tell them to fire a couple of warning shots once they get in eyesight. That should buy us a couple more minutes. And tell Alexis and Killah to take their squads and flank them as soon as they are all within range. Just the same as we practiced. We want to surround these bastards."

"Gotcha!" the young woman said shaking her head to let him know that she understood before turning and heading down the steps.

"What's this all about Moses?"

"I'm not sure and I don't want to speculate but I think we're about to find out. You ready?"

"Born ready baby. Let's get these bastards!"

"Listen woman. I want you and my son behind me. I don't want you out there acting like you some super woman. Do you hear me woman?" Moses said glaring at the woman in front of him.

"I hear you love," Maya replied a little surprised by Moses' tone. She couldn't remember him ever being this assertive.

Moses was still struggling with his suspenders when the mob rode up. The warning from the sentries startling them into almost a rout but they recovered quickly. They were only too surprised to find these ex-slaves armed to the teeth, dug in, and ready for battle when they arrived. Moses rode out a few paces beyond the perimeter his rifle cradled against his chest.

"Evening gentleman! May I inquire as to the nature of your visit to New Eden at such a late hour?" Moses' big, baritone voice boomed out across the divide.

It was the older gentleman who'd incited the men who now took a swig from his jug who spoke first.

"What we want nigga is the bitch that runs this outfit."

"That would be me," replied Maya who rode up from the shadows.

"I thought I asked you to stay back," Moses said chiding the woman who now stood by his side.

"The man asked for me Moses," Maya said smiling.

"You're the reason me and my boys is outta work and we're here to string your Black ass up. We'll teach you to know your place nigga," he shouted.

Before anyone could utter another word, Moses had come to the decision that the man's words were somehow not quite appropriate when addressing a female. And raising his rifle Moses shot the man striking him squarely between the eyes. The man fell from his horse with a thud and neither his men or the residents of New Eden moved. A pin could be heard.

"It is unfortunate that had to happen but no man worth his salt addresses a woman in that manner," Moses said letting the mob know that he had no tolerance for vigilante justice.

"Thank you m'love and I am sorry if any of you feel that I'm responsible for your being out of work but if any of you think you can stomach working alongside of a niggra then be here at 6 a.m. I have plenty of work and let it be known that I pay more than the going rate." Maya said.

"Now let's get on home," Moses said following up. "6 a.m. will be here before you know it. You're late you don't work," Moses said to the mob still in shock over their fallen leader. Not more than an hour later all had returned to normal among the residents of New Eden or so it seemed.

"They'll be back."

"Yes, but how will they be back is the question. They could come back with the constable lookin' for m'baby for killin' a white man."

"That's certainly one scenario," Moses countered.

"Then they could just have a delayed reaction and double back seeking revenge or some other nonsense. You notice they'd been drinking, didn't you?"

"Yeah, that was pretty apparent. I think I sobered 'em up though." Moses smiled.

"That you did m'love. You stood up there and protected my honor and every other woman's honor here at New Eden," Maya said grabbing Moses hands in hers. But then again if it's really about feeding their families then we should see a good many of them in the morning."

"Do you understand what I was telling you about pushing too hard. You've worked these crackers into a frenzy."

"I'm sorry but I have to disagree with you m'love. I think the good Lord put me here and gave me certain talents just like he imparts his blessings on everyone. When a white man does the same thing, nothing is said. Why do you put limits on me?"

"Because you are not a white man and the repercussions for all of us could be devastating. Them crackers came with the intent of lynching you. Presently we are wealthy beyond our means. Our folks are doin' better than most white folks. Their homes rival the nicest homes in Boston. We have plans for a school and so many other things. But we don't want to incense our neighbors. Stop trying to monopolize and diversify. Open the bakery and the restaurant. Open a cleaners and a boutique. With your savvy you can be a success in any avenue you choose to travel. You can make the same if not more money without cornering the market and driving folks out of business."

"I hear you Moses. I'll keep that in mind. You know if I had my way I'd drive all them crackers out of business and just have to live with the fallout."

"Is that where Alexis gets her bitterness from?"

Maya was forced to laugh.

"Let's go bed. I have a feeling tomorrow's going to be one trying day m'love."

"Let's pray it's not," Moses replied kissing Maya on the forehead before rolling over.

"Did you double the sentries on duty?"

"Tripled them."

"Thank you m'love. You know I love you, don't you?"

"I love you more. Good night."

The next morning the sun played peek-a-boo not quite sure if it should rise or not. Moses felt the same way finally getting up and giving thanks and praise to the almighty Allah for not sending another attack or the law with orders to arrest him during the night. Lord knows he had tried to warn Maya. There was enough to go around. What was her real motive for her wanting to show her dominance and authority? Was it her need to exact revenge and make white folks pay for the indignities she'd endured all her life? What else could it be? Now a man was dead and he not she was responsible. And there was so much more than what transpired last night. I had a son on the way and from what the doctors have indicated she should have already have had him but knowing Maya she probably just told him to wait until she finished her business. I hadn't said a word up until this point. I was content to sit by and wait patiently but the doctors said that if she would just relax and recommended bed rest. I knew that wasn't happening and what could I tell a woman that's done this fourteen times already.

Moses was surprised to find a long line of white men lined up at with Maya interviewing each man.

"I'm paying you, but I don't want no problems and no regrets. Do you understand? If you can't stomach workin' with niggras we don't want, you here. How you feel about that suh? You think you can work under those terms?"

"I ain't got nothing against no man be he colored or white as long as he's a man. How they say it? I respect those who respect themselves."

"I like that. What's your name suh?"

"David ma'am. What's yours?"

"You can just refer to me as ma'am. Works for me David."

"Okay David and what as it you did on your last job?"

"Nothing much. I was foreman ma'am."

"Okay David. Step to the right. The older gentlemen there will get you started. Who's next?"

This went on time after time.

"There were certainly more men than rode in here last night," Maya commented after interviewing all eighty-six men.

"Word spreads quickly when a man is out of work."

"Watch them closely for the first month or so. Put two sets of eyes on each one of them and make sure they weren't put here."

"I do believe ol' man Johnson already took care of that."

"Oh, and that's why I love you so. You're always a step ahead of me. It is so nice not have to carry the weight of this entire clan on my shoulders anymore," Maya said before grabbing Moses and holding him. And then she yelled and fell her head nearly missing the dining room table just as Elise stepped in. Stepping out just as quickly the young woman was as cool as she ever was. Only once had he seen her unhinged.

"Grab her legs, Moses. Let's get her upstairs and into bed."

Shortly thereafter Moses sat in the library pretending to check the books when Elise walked in.

"You look like you've seen a ghost. Are you okay Moses."

"I'm fine," he stuttered. "I just can't understand how all of you are so calm with her screaming like that."

Elise had to laugh.

"Come on Moses. I'm the oldest of her children. I don't know how many times I've seen this before. Only this time she's happy. And you have nothing to worry about. Mommy's one of the strongest women I know."

"I pray you're right."

Before Elise had a chance to answer the sound of gunfire pierced the August evening. Both he and Elise jumped and headed for the door. Off in the distance and despite the dissipating sun Moses could make out a crowd of men. Armed men were coming from their homes in droves now in response to the shots and assumed their positions along the perimeter. Moses grabbed his horse and rode out to see what the commotion was all about. The sentries had done their job laying down just enough to keep the men at bay until reinforcements lined their foxholes.

"I don't want no trouble with you niggas. I just want one thing and me and my brothers will be out of here."

"What that's young fella? What's that one thing that I can get for you?"

"My brother's and me want the man that killed my father."

"I don't believe I know your father."

"Don't play with me nigga."

"I do believe that type of language is what got your father in trouble."

"Then you knew my father. I'm the one that killed him," Moses said pointing the rifle at the young man. "And if you don't want the same thing to happen to you and your brothers I suggest you get the hell off my land."

"See what my brothers have to say about this, but I can promise you it won't be pretty."

"I can guarantee you it won't be pretty," Moses replied as the man turned and rode off.

Moses rode the entire perimeter.

"Folks, today we send a message. Shoot to maim not to kill. We want them to go home and say those niggas ain't to be messed with. That's the message we want to send."

I didn't have time to mess with these crackers tonight. With Maya in labor I needed to be by her side or at least in the house since those meddlesome old women wouldn't allow me to be by her side.

"Elise. I need you to ride and inform the constable that these man are on our land making threats and accusations and there looks to be bloodshed."

As soon as she rode off Moses sent for Alexis.

"Hey sweetie. I need for you to handle this situation," Moses said grabbing the young woman by the shoulders and staring straight into her eyes.

"I want a clear message sent to these crackers and any of their buddies who think it's alright to ride up in here and try to harass us. I want a clear message sent that the niggras form New Eden are not to be messed with. I chose you to lead this because I want it done right. Where hoods if necessary but not under any circumstances do I want any one killed. Is that understood?"

The smile rapidly turned into a frown, but Alexis agreed. After all orders were orders.

"I gotcha. Now you get on in there with mommy. I got this old man," Alexis said winking at Moses before turning and riding towards her men. Moses had to smile. The woman would most likely be famous if there had been a war to fight. If there was place she shone above all others it was the battlefield. The art of killing came second nature to her. Still, he knew that out of all Maya's children Alexis was the one that would take his orders and fill them out to a tee even if she wasn't in complete agreement. And she only had one result when it came to warring white folk. Kill them all and never have to worry about that particular problem again.

Moses was greeted on the steps of the house with news of a beautiful baby boy. Elated he ran, taking two steps at a time until he was by Maya's side.

"I wasn't sure I wanted to have your son after I heard the gunshots. Will we never have any peace, Moses. I seriously thought we left all this behind."

"I did too," Moses said grinning from ear-to-ear holding his son ever so gently. "He's beautiful."

"Yes, he is," Maya said taking the baby from Moses. "So, what's this latest little commotion about?"

"Nothing for you to worry your pretty little head about. What I need for you to do is to rest. Can you do that for me?" Moses said bending over to kiss Maya his eyes never leaving his newborn son. "Just beautiful," he remarked to no one in particular. It was more or less a revelation.

Outside he was surprised to find the same scenario he'd left.

"What's going on Alexis?"

"Exactly what you see. I don't know if they sent for reinforcements or they're scouting us. I could have chased them home but with you sending for the law and all I figured we needed to be in the right. I didn't want to be the one that provoked it by firing the first shot."

"That's why I left you in charge," Moses said hugging his nineteen-year-old daughter who grinned as widely as he did. There was nothing better than receiving Moses' approval at least not to Alexis who had grown to love her stepfather dearly.

Pretending to ignore the remark Alexis turned the conversation to other things.

"Did those ol' witches allow you to see your son?"

"He's beautiful," Moses said beaming brightly.

"I'm sure," Alexis replied.

"Why don't you rush up to the house and take a gander. I think I can manage this until you get back."

"I think I'll just do that. They don't know it, but they're completely surrounded. It's hopeless. We need to send someone out there and let them know and tell them to go home before they're all killed," Alexis said.

"Don't tell me you're getting soft in your old age. A couple of months ago I would have come out of the house and the gravediggers would have been hiding any evidence," Moses teased.

"This wouldn't have even been a fight. More like a massacre. There's no point."

"And since when did that matter. I do remember you going into battle screaming 'no mercy, no quarters'. Moses reminded the young woman.

"Unfortunately, that's true. And I fear I will have to answer to my God for my indiscretions. I am not looking forward to that day."

"I don't believe any of us are. Go see the baby. You're starting to depress me."

Before Moses could finish there was a loud pop. Alexis head turned, and Moses could see the smoke coming from her temple where the bullet was lodged.

She fell to the ground screaming 'Moses' name but he knew that she was gone before she hit the ground. Moses left the comfort of his shelter and headed right into a hail of bullets. He no longer was concerned with his welfare. He had one concern now. He wanted to kill every last one of those crackers who killed his Alexis.

The New Eden soldiers followed Moses lead and laid down a penetrating fire that had those crackers looking for avenues of retreat but there was nowhere to go as Black faces formed a tighter and tighter circle. There had been no more than thirty men in all. Now there were only eight left when Moses asked ol' man Johnson for his axe and in plain view of everyone chopped down each of those men before turning and walking back to Alexis' limp, lifeless body. Picking her up gently, the tears running from his eyes Moses took the girl in and placed her on the sofa in the parlor before heading up to the bedroom to inform Maya who sensed something wrong as soon as Moses walked in the room. Call it a women's intuition.

"Moses! What's wrong?!" she screamed loud enough for everyone in the house to hear.

A deeply troubled and tormented Moses moved to his wife's side. His anger mixed with a feeling of loss and sorrow remained foremost within him.

"Who is it, Moses!? Oh, God I knew this day would come. I've always known this day would come. Death is unavoidable in warfare. Who was it?" Maya asked the tears flowing freely down her cheeks.

"Alexis," Moses said barely above a whisper. He was weeping openly now. There was no mistaking and as much as he loved them all for their distinctive personalities it was always Alexis with her buoyant personality that would keep a smile on your face. And not that he would ever admit to but Alexis was his clear favorite.

'And now this. And for what? Damn to hell all of those crackers that hate me merely because of the color of my skin! Damn them all to hell. Now my poor child is only a memory because of this senseless violence. Damn you all to hell.' Moses thoughts were all jumbled. He was doing his best to reach center again and become the rock he had chosen to be but right now he was having problems centering himself. He was still too angry. He'd lost one of his charges, a daughter, confidante at times but always a loyal and trustworthy friend. And in his moment of grief he could not remember how many he'd laid to rest in her name but somehow it did not seem like nearly enough.

"The Good Lord giveth and the Good Lord taketh away," Maya said handing the baby to one of the midwives standing bedside. "Somehow I always knew it would be her," Maya said before dropping her head to her chest and letting the tears flow.

The room was beginning to swell with both family and friends. Nineteen-year-old Alexis had long ago taken the role of protectorate of the folks now of New Eden. They both loved and respected the fiery little redbone who was never without her captivating smile and never had an ill word for anyone. And now just like that she was gone.

Elise and Maya held each other both sobbing openly while Killah held his mother's hand with the hopes of giving her strength or perhaps in hopes of receiving it. To say it was a most trying time for everyone would be an understatement. But Maya proved strong scheduling the funeral and christening back-to-back on the same day. Condolences from within and without New Eden and from Boston proper came in by the droves and Maya was surprisingly upbeat despite the funeral. Crowds of folks gathered on the front lawn to pay their respects, but Maya was oblivious.

"Moses."

"Yes, dear."

"I've decided that I want to be married this week. Nothing too big just family."

"That's big," Moses joked.

The following Saturday the two were formally married under the old oak in the front yard. Old man Johnson a self-ordained minister performed the ceremony while Elise acted as maid-of-honor and Killah served as best man. It was just as Maya planned it. Quiet. And the reception turned out to be nothin' more than just another Sunday dinner with all the family gathered round the dinner table.

They named the baby Paul. Maya said it had something to do with them leaving that land of evil and the Good Lord turning things topsy-turvy where

Colored folks was no longer slaves but free to the man. She somehow got it all convoluted and reckons that the story of Saul in the bible with his revelation that made him change his ways and his name from Saul to Paul. This revelation to Paul was the same type of revelation that Maya saw her destiny move from slavery to freedom and he who had been under the heavy, guise of slavery was now free like Saul changing to Paul. It was just that simple, just that easy. Have Maya tell it though the parable took on a whole new and different tint when it came to her son Paul being the first of her fifteen born free. Maya would tell anyone who asked.

'I believe the way I rightly recollect Saul was on the road from Damascus collecting for the pharisees when he bumped into the Good Lord who asked him in no uncertain terms the way only the Good Lord can do.

'Saul please tell me what in the hell you're doing to your brothers and sisters, my children? You must know that you are doing the devil's bidding?'

Saul was so shocked that the Lord had seen fit to confront him on this dusty, dirt road leading nowhere that he fell off his horse landing face first in the mud. He lay there still, not moving, nor did he say a word. The Good Lord was not pleased with this response being that he felt compelled to take time out of his busy schedule to deal with this idiot so he asked him once again in a much-beleaguered tone.

'Do you hear me talking to you son?'

'Yes sir. I mean your honor. Uh sir,' Saul stuttered not sure what to call the entity in front of him.

'Now back to the question at hand. Are you not aware of the fact that you are causing your brothers and sisters, my children great pain and heartache with the pharisees demands? Hasn't that occurred to you?'

Saul shook his head. He knew. But the money was right, and he had to admit he liked the sense of power it gave him. Yet, if the Good Lord was making a special trip to just see and admonish him then he'd better make a change and make it fast before being faced with hell and damnation. No, he did not want that. And if wasn't a believer he was now.

'I promise I will do better m'Lord.'

'I sincerely hope son. I would hate to think this is going to be an ongoing issue. Sometimes it's important to make a change in our lives. And keep this in mind. You can profit financially, or you can profit spiritually. At the end of the day see which one makes you feel whole?'

It was that meeting that opened Saul's eyes. He even went so far as to change his name from Saul to Paul divorcing himself completely from his previous life.

Maya saw her son, the first to be born wealthy and free to inherit a new world but was interrupted by Moses' mood as of late.

"Husband," she said sitting downstairs in the library with the hopes of sharing time with Moses who sat brooding again. These days Moses could be found sitting somewhere alone his thoughts whirling out of control.

"Listen to me my husband. I need you to snap out of it! Believe me I understand your grief, but you cannot let it consume you. You cannot allow it to make you bitter."

"I'm most certain that this same woman who's every intent is trying to run roughshod over every cracker she comes into contact with leaving them barely hanging on to dear life and one step from the grave is surely not lecturing me on becoming bitter," Moses said the anger and annoyance obvious in his tone.

"That's not fair Moses. You didn't grow up a slave. You didn't grow up being raped every time the massa felt the need or got the whim. You've never been made to watch your own daughter be raped and ravaged by her own father on a drunken binge. She killed him you know?"

"No, I didn't know and frankly I wish you hadn't told me. But since we're on the subject of baby girl want to share something with you that she shared with me before she…" Moses became so caught up that his eyes welled with tears as he reflected on the last thing Alexis with tears said to him before being killed.

"I was teasing Alexis about coming in and seeing the baby and returning and there were still men left standing. And she told me in all earnestness that there had been too much killing already and she was afraid that she was going to be held accountable and be made to atone for her sins."

"She told you that?!"

"Yes, she did. Right before she was shot and killed."

"Then He forgave her!"

"That's the way I see it too. Once she came around to see the folly of her deeds and regret them that was enough for Him to call another one of his angels home."

"Why didn't you tell me this before now?"

"I'm still coming to grasp with it. I haven't been able to talk about it. It's a sensitive subject."

"Be honest with me Moses so I can better understand. Out of all my children she was your favorite wasn't she. And don't give me that mess about how you can never choose a favorite among your children. That's my line. She was your favorite, wasn't she? And to think I always thought it was Jeremiah."

"Yes, she was my favorite. It would lift my spirits every time I saw her smiling face and you know as well as I do she affected everyone she came into contact with the same way. She was a special soul that comes along and only briefly once in a lifetime. She's like a shooting star He graces you with for just a moment before calling her back home. How can one not brood when he considers that she is gone forever?"

"No one is hurt any deeper than I am. And it's alright to brood. That I understand. I am brooding and grieving her as well. She was that shooting star and so it will take some time, but it is no excuse for you to become bitter. That's all I'm saying. But do you know why I am able to cope with it? Because I have faith in the Lord and He knows what is best. So strong is my faith in him that I can lay this burden at His feet and continue on with my life and with my other children and husband who all need me in some way or fashion. I have to maintain the strength and again it is He who endows me with that strength."

"I apologize but my faith is not that strong," Moses admitted the tears flowing freely.

"It will be my husband. It will be," Maya said kissing the top of Moses' pate.

"By the way, have you happened to see my son in the last seventy-two hours?"

"No, I haven't but I'm quite sure he's fine. He's a novelty right now and they're spoilin' the heck out of him of that you can be sure. Stop your worrying. I'm sure one of the kids has him and well they're all pretty responsible." Maya said hoping to curb Moses fear.

"I'm not worried. I have faith in you and I know how you are when it comes to the little ones. I'm just tryna recollect what the little fella looks like."

"Looks like a baby all wrinkled and shriveled up."

"See you're okay with this because you've done this whole children thing once or twice before, excuse me if my math's a little off but I am a first-time father. Could you see if you can locate him and have him come stand in a line up and see if I can recognize the traveling child."

"I'll put out an APB with haste my love," Maya smiled.

"Well, if you ever feel a loss for your child feel free to kidnap and adopt one of these others. Trust me I have enough that you should never be at a loss."

This time it was Moses' turn to smile.

"Elise you must have known I was thinking about you."

"Oh no, that's not good. What evil deed do you need me to carry out now mommy?"

Maya grinned broadly pushing her cheekbones as high as they would go.

"I know you were thinking about me so much you've been having me followed? What are you thinking mommy?"

"Now, now, Elise slow your roll girl before you completely misconstrue my intentions. I did it for your protection, baby. I don't trust these crackers. They killed your sister and would have no problem killing you as well. And now that the word has spread about New Eden there's an ever-increasing chance of a kidnapping. These rich niggas at New Eden has got their attention so weez gots ta be careful young'un," Maya said grabbing her oldest daughter and hugging her tightly. "Can't let nothin' happen to my favorite daughter," she said whispering and looking around and making sure no one else was listening. Maya told all her children the same thing when she had them alone. And to her each one of them was her favorite with each having their own very special and unique features.

"I gotcha mommy but next time you send someone you may want to send someone a little more inconsp

"Why you wanna lie 'Lise. You didn't know I was there and I suggest you hush before I tell mommy what I saw," he grinned.

"Stop right now you two," Maya said sternly. Not another word was spoken.

"Hold on mommy. I've got to tell you this one. One day your son thought he'd lost me and, in his haste, to find me ran straight into me. When I asked him what he was doing and where he was going he just stood there babbling," Elise teased.

"Elise will you stop teasing your brother."

"I will if you tell me why you're so dressed up mommy. You have something special planned."

"Well, yes I do now that you mention it I'm taking Moses on the honeymoon that he never had."

"From the looks of little Paul it looks like you've been honeymooning the whole way here," Elise laughed and even Killah who rarely smiled had to chuckle at his sister's comment.

"I'm going to pretend I didn't hear that and Killah I'd appreciate it if you wouldn't feed into her utter disrespect and lack of tact. Seriously though I'm going to need you to go over the books, see where we can cut costs and increase profits. Killah I want you to get those men working on the mill to speed up. The longer the mill is down we're losing more money than you know. Get three shifts working 'round the clock but get it finished. Then I need either of you or both of you to check on the businesses downtown, including the boutique and the bakery. Spend some time and get a feel for how they're doing. Then do the same thing at the restaurant."

"Goodness mommy. You make it sound like you're going to be gone for some time."

"Just a few days."

"And who's going with you?"

"I do believe I said we were going on our honeymoon. That would consist of one husband Moses and his very elegant wife Maya. I do believe that's all that's needed sweetie pie," she said kissing Elise on her forehead.

"Oh no! Not after that speech I just heard on the dangers that now confront the residents of New Eden. It all makes perfect sense which is why I'm sending an armed escort with you and believe me you won't know there there," Elise said smiling at her mother. "And don't worry, not that you're worried cause Miss Maya knows she raised her children to be mature, responsible adults but Katharine and I have Paul. Other people try to get him but Kathy and me form a pretty formidable tandem. I think Kathy broke one of your other children's noses. Might have been Dada's. I wasn't there but he tried to come in the house forcibly and she cracked him a good one. Broke his nose. He's been in the house since then. Ain't really had no one else try to come and get him since then. Think she sent a message."

"You tell him I want to see him pronto. And what? You're just going to adopt my son? His father said if they put him in a line up he's not sure he could point him out. Can he at least get visitation rights?"

Both Killah and Elise fell out.

"Is it really that bad?"

"How long have you had him?"

"Let me see," Elise said smiling broadly. "About three weeks."

"The boy's only a month-old Elise."

By this time Elise and her brother were in tears.

"I kept wondering why I hadn't seen you."

"You know how it is mommy. I o to work, to school and then home. That's it," Elise said doing her best to hold a straight face. "That's my life in the nutshell."

"And kidnapping. Add that to the list."

"C'mon mommy he's as much ours as he is yours. And all we want is the same thing that you want and that's to see him grow up to be a proud, strong Black man just my like big brother here," she said grabbing Killah from behind in a bear hug of sorts. Anyway, no need for worry. Baby boy's in good hands. He's in my hands."

Maya nodded in compliance.

"Moses come on. We have reservations for eight and it's almost seven now. You know it's a good hours ride," Maya shouted.

Not long after the two rode into Boston Proper or Roxbury in the finest Paris fall wear accompanied by Elise and six of New Eden's most elite guard. Procuring the nicest suite in the Roxbury Hotel Maya noticed only one thing in the lavish suite. Moses. And with no further ado she took her man, this man Moses, her husband over and over and over again until the moon gave way to the sun.

Morning came long before Maya or Moses had any intentions of getting up. Maya had hoped to pick up where she'd left off the night before but all the commotion in the street below somehow just wouldn't allow it. Maya turned over on the bed and glanced through the daily paper while Moses peered out the window at the commotion below.

"Did you know that a mob attacked Mr. Douglass and William Lloyd Garrison after a meeting they had the other night right here in Boston."

"You sound surprised. Racism is everywhere. It's woven into the very fabric that we call America. There are enough racists here to cause trouble but, in the end, good will always prevail over evil. But listen that's Elise and some white man causin' all that commotion. I'm gonna run down and see what all this is about."

"I'm coming with you," Maya said grabbing her petticoat.

Fully dressed in the new brown suit Maya had ordered from New York Moses portrayed a very well-to-do gentleman. Strapping on his pistols Maya turned to the six-foot gentleman now by her side.

"Do you really think those are necessary sweetheart?"

"I hope not but I've always made it a point to plan for the unexpected especially when dealing with white folks. You ready?"

"I'm ready for you my husband," Maya teased. "Why don't you let me relax you and let Elise handle it?"

"Cause I can't afford to lose another child to some crazy cracker," Moses said before storming out of the room only to find Elise and Phoenix embroiled in a bitter dispute.

"You have no reason to deny me entry into this hotel young lady," the rather robust, gentleman with the thick mustache shouted.

"I told you that they are on their honeymoon and our job is to make sure that they not be disturbed. If it's concerning business, then you can speak to me. I am authorized to handle all business dealings."

"Are you the proprietor of M&M Lumber? That is who I wish to speak to."

"And you can speak to the proprietor during normal business hours which are Monday through Friday between nine and five," Elise retorted.

"Morning sweetie," Moses said kissing Elise and Phoenix on both cheeks before turning to the irate man.

"Is there something I can do for you sir?"

"Yes, I'd like to speak to the proprietor of M&M Lumber. I understand they're staying here."

"You're speaking to the proprietor of M&M Lumber."

"Excuse my husband but you are speaking to the proprietors of M&M," Maya chimed in letting her presence be known.

"Maya why don't you and I grab a table. I hear they have a fabulous breakfast and I'm famished," Moses said putting his arm proudly around his new wife.

"I'm sorry I don't do business with women."

"And I believe my daughter informed you that the missus and I are on our honeymoon and we are not to be disturbed. She also gave you our normal business hours. I hope to hear from you then. Good day sir."

Moses seated Maya and then himself only to find the man still standing there chuckling to himself at which time Moses put his hand on his pistol under the table. By now Maya had come to notice the subtle movement and placed her hand on top of his. It would be easy to let him blow this cracker that didn't know how to take no for an answer, but it was too soon after Alexis' death and she knew Moses had no problem blowing away any white man without the slightest provocation. She had to help her man through this phase of the whole grieving process. She knew he was both grieving and angry and the slightest provocation from any white man could quickly lead to his death and this man was clearly pushing it.

"By the way, I didn't get your name?"

"Kilpatrick. James Kilpatrick. And I don't know if you know it or not but you're the talk of the town. In less than a year I have witnessed the small lumberyards go out of business one by one. And do you know why they went under?"

"Okay! It's time you leave sir," Moses said rising from his seat. Maya grabbed him pulling him back to his seat.

"Let the man speak Moses. I'm curious to see where he's going with this. Proceed. Mr. Kilpatrick is it?"

"The reason those businesses went under was because you undercut them and stole their business."

"Excuse me sir but as I understand it this is America and America is based on capitalism which fosters competitiveness. What happens is a lot of competitors choose to enter the race and find out they really can't compete, and they bow out. It's simply the nature of the game. But I think we're all aware of that going in. Wouldn't you agree?"

"That's very true but as owner of two of the largest lumberyards in Massachusetts I know that there is enough to go around and it's important that you allow the smaller mom and pop joints to eat. Our aim is not to harm our neighbors in helping ourselves. You see now that you have overstepped your bounds they have all come running to me. That's when I'm forced to step in and that's also when things tend to get ugly. And we don't want that now do we? Then what I strongly suggest you might want to consider are your neighbors and competition and you may want to slow your plans for expansion and steamrolling all competition. And your plans for the docks which would cement your monopolization of the lumber business in the Boston area is henceforth terminated. I hope that it's understood that the M&M Lumber company will place no bid for control of the docks. Names Kilpatrick. Ask around about me before you make a decision."

And with said the tall, handsome, man turned to leave. Moses could see Maya's mood change, her anger rising with each of Kilpatrick's words. The tables had turned, and it was Moses who now patiently tapped on Maya's leg with the hopes of defusing the situation, but Moses soon learned his efforts had been in vain.

"Mr. Kilpatrick I would hate to tell you what happened to the last man that threatened me."

"It was nice to have met you ma'am," Kilpatrick said smiling before tipping his hat and making his leave. Moses was up and out of his seat as soon as he saw Kilpatrick up on his horse.

"Elise, I want you to follow him. Keep a safe distance but I need to know where he goes, who he knows. I need to know everything you can find out about him. Ask around but be careful."

"Will do. I'll check in with you later this evening."

When Moses returned to the table he found Maya in her own little world and did not feel compelled to disturb her.

"You know when she was a little girl he would ask so many questions like how come white folks could buy and sell Black people. And how come Black folks get treated like animals. I couldn't answer it then and I can't answer it now," Maya said the tears flowing down both brown cheeks. "Please tell me white folks ain't the same everywhere?"

"Wish I could. Sorry to say that there's a faction of racism everywhere I've been in this here America."

"And there's nowhere to go to rid ourselves of this racist element?"

"No," Moses said hugging his wife as she sobbed quietly in his arms. He only wished he could somehow eliminate the pain of racism that so tormented her and niggras as a whole and that had always grieved her so.

Moses and Maya spent the remainder of the day in bed she reading Adam Smith's A Wealth of Nations and he bored out of his mind glancing the daily rag. At times Maya would read a few pages and then stare out of the big bay window her mind obviously elsewhere.

"She had so many questions Moses and her questions would so enrage me. Not because they weren't valid questions but because I had no answers for them. And I still don't have any answers for them," Maya said to everyone and no one in particular. "You know why that cracker approached us today?"

"Have no idea," Moses said not looking up from the paper.

"What did he forbid us from bidding on?"

"The docks. He knows that whoever controls the docks controls the city's lumber contract for the next ten years. He knows that the person that gets that contract can close up shop and retire off that alone and that cracker is determined not to let a nigga gain control of the docks."

Both were silent for now. Moses spelled it out.

"So, my husband what would you suggest I do?" Maya asked.

"Concerning the docks? If you just give me some time say until this evening I can better advise you. I sent Elise on a little fact-finding mission. I think we can get a better idea of who and what we're dealing with when she returns. It's important that we know the enemy before we engage him. We must first know our enemy."

"Well, while we're waiting for the scouting report why don't you come over here and relax your wife who so badly needs you."

Moses placed both hands on Maya's back and gently began massaging her. She adored this. In a matter of minutes, she was fast asleep. And after reading for a little over an hour Moses found himself getting just a tad bit claustrophobic. After all, Maya had had him under house arrest for the past three days. What he needed was some fresh air, some new surroundings. But for right now a stiff drink would suffice. Dressing quickly and quietly he did his best not to wake Maya. He loved his wife dearly, but she could be overwhelming at times with her constant bequests. Sadly, enough this was the only time he saw her relax.

Moses took the stairs before heading across the main lobby and straight for the crowded bar. He was pleasantly surprised find his drinking partner ol'man Johnson posted up at the bar with all the focus being on the old man. He was a character alright and one of the smartest men that Moses knew.

"Johns," Moses shouted in an attempt to get the old man's attention.

"Moses. Hey man how you been?" the old man said grabbing and hugging Moses. He was genuinely glad to see his old drinkin' partner. The two men hadn't really had a chance to get together since they'd come off the trail and the ol'man chose to live on the very outskirts of New Eden a good four or five miles away from Moses' residence. Little did the old man know that it was he who Moses sought out and who had more often not given him the strength and motivation to keep going on the trail when he was doubting himself. Moses loved the old man and held him in the highest regard.

"It's good to see you Moses."

The two had formed a bond on the trail and become family. They all had.

"It's good to see you as well, Johns. I've been meaning to stop by and see how you were getting' along but my new massa is worse than the old one and doesn't allow me to stray too far from the nest."

Johns couldn't help but laugh.

"I've known Maya practically all her life and anyone that knows her knows she's high maintenance. You knew that. I just wish you would have come and seen me before you tied the knot. I could have warned you."

Both men laughed.

"So, what brings you here, Johns?"

"I should ask you that. This is my usual watering hole. I like to come here to see how the other half is living. What are you doing here?"

"You already know."

Johns chuckled.

"What are you drinking?" Moses asked still grinning broadly.

"House whiskey."

"Two Jack Daniels please. Make those doubles," Moses said shouting over others.

"So, how have you been my friend?"

"Fair-to-middlin'. Ain't really got no reason to complain."

"No. I guess not after what we just accomplished. That was quite a journey and it didn't come without it's challenges and we withstood them all. That's quite an accomplishment for a bunch of slaves. Fought off all comers and suffered little or no casualties. I'd say that is quite an accomplishment. Here's to you son," Johns said raising his glass.

"Couldn't have done it without you. It was rocky at points, but I think we handled it pretty well overall."

"I heard about the killing of baby girl. I know how you felt about her. That was a real tragedy. She was one feisty little fireball she was. And you know out of all of Maya's children to me she was the one that most resembled her mother. She had that same relentless spirit. Tell me. How's Maya holding up?"

Well considering everything she's been unbelievable. Strongest woman I've ever met. She's on me for brooding. Tell me something Johns. How often do you come here?"

"Once or twice a week when Sarah meets with her knitting club. Why do you ask?"

"So, you're privy to all the talk around town?"

"Pretty much. What's up?"

"You ever hear talk of a James Kilpatrick?"

"Never heard nothin' good. He comes in here from time-to-time but he ain't no friend of the Coloreds. He's got some money and political ties downtown. They say he owns the land and every general store for the next three counties. He ain't nothing to be toyed with and he will resort to violence at the drop of a hat. My advice is to stay clear of him. Why do you ask?"

"He came at Maya and me this morning telling her not to bid on the docks."

"Then you don't bid on the docks. Our community is already thriving. Thanks to you and Maya we are doing better than any of us could ever have imagined and if she's doing this for the sake of New Eden then I suggest that she let it go. You have to ask yourself how much is enough? New Eden can rival any upper-class community in Boston. We're thriving without the docks. So, we let it go and continue to grow and prosper until we have the strength to stand up to the James Kilpatrick's of the world but I'm afraid we're not quite there yet. But one day we will be."

"You're preachin' to the choir but I'm not the one who felt disrespected and demeaned."

"Tell her I said to swallow her ego. One insult is not worth burying a whole community and if Maya decides to bid on the docks that's exactly what she'll be doing. Kilpatrick is mean as a snake and quite capable of doing just that, burying New Eden.

Those folks at New Eden worked hard and walked a long way to get to the Promised Land. We are all lucrative and have more than we ever thought possible. Don't allow her to throw away all the hard work we put in Moses."

"I hear you and believe me I agree with you one hundred percent the problem is that isn't my concern nor my choice to make. And don't forget who we are talking about. This is Maya who believes that no white man would come under the scrutiny that they have subjected her to."

"And she's absolutely right. Because the war ended slavery and declared Colored folks free don't mean they equal. And she's too bright a woman not to know that."

"I'm pretty sure Maya understands that, but Maya doesn't think there's anything to live for if there's nothing to die for and I would wholeheartedly agree if her ego would just allow herself to be a victim of martyrdom, but her ego cannot and should not be allowed to destroy what the good folks of New Eden have given so much for. I hear you and agree with you my friend."

"Then talk to her man," Johns said with all the passion to be had. He was serious. And he had never known Johns to miss a good fight. He was always on the front lines directing but this man Kilpatrick scared Johns. And he was not only advising but stressing that Maya didn't engage. There was no hemmin' and hawin' or we could possibly try this. No. This was an emphatic no that suggested that there was no room for discussion from a man he respected and followed in times of war.

"I'll do that Johns," Moses said pouring down the rest of his whiskey.

"Talk to her for all of us. C'mon let me buy the next round."

"I ain't foolin' with' you Johns. You'll have me plumb drunk and Maya will have my head. I told you we were on our honeymoon," Moses said almost pleading now.

"I still don't see how you let that old woman corral you boy. Shit, she 'bout my age and I'll be seventy-three my next birthday. I know because they had a special parade the year I was born and so I went to the library and looked up the parade and that's how I found out the year I was born. I don't know why it was so important to me, but it was. But anyway, be honest with me. I mean we friends ain't we?"

"Yeah, I suppose we are why?"

"Then I want you to be honest with me?"

"Go ahead. Shoot Johns."

"Then please tell me why you married that old woman?"

This caused Moses to spit his drink out and double over in laughter.

"You a fool Johns."

"Not only did you marry this spinster but the fact that she has fourteen children should have been a small clue to run the other way. Fourteen kids! Not one or two. Not even three or four but fourteen. What the hell did she offer? King Tut's tomb. Probably some distant relative. She hit you with that thing that got her fourteen kids and you said what the hell. Doesn't hurt that she's rich beyond her wildest means and has distributed the wealth nicely. Or could it be that you've simply fallen in love m'boy?"

"I think I've just fallen in love," Moses acknowledged.

"Well, all jokes aside Moses you couldn't fallen for a more handsome woman and one of the brightest women I've had the occasion to come across. Now you run along before she comes down here lookin' for you and catches me. You know how women talk."

"Good seein' ya Johns," Moses said hugging his dear friend.

"I want you to stop by and have supper with me and Martha this week. We eat at six. The same time every night," the old man said.

"I will make it a priority."

"We always have a good laugh don't we Moses?"

"Yes, we do Johns," Moses said before making his way through the crowd and to the stairs.

"Enjoy your honeymoon. It's all downhill after that," Johns yelled.

Entering the room, he was surprised to find Maya still asleep. Hearing him walking around she awoke and he was quickly on her neck nuzzling like a horse in a bag of oats. This was her weak spot and she giggled uncontrollably as he continued to nuzzle her neck when she turned on her back he was on top spreading her legs with his own before entering her quickly and deeply and riding her to the verge of one delicious orgasm before he pulled up. She gasped. He was teasing her again. He had plans on knocking her out. He'd tease her until she was begging him to let her cum. But it wasn't until she was sweating profusely and shaking uncontrollably that he would allow her to bust in showering waves of purples and pinks. There was nothing left but a gracious smile and sleep at which time he would conduct his own private affairs. They both knew this, but she was not relinquishing this pleasure for an inkling with no foundation.

"I'm just telling you what Johns said Maya. And you know as well as I do that he has always been a more than reliable source. And he's not saying or even trying to come up with a viable strategy to beat

him. He's saying concede or risk losing everything,

and his concern is primarily for the folks of New

Eden."

"And his own."

"And his own but is one contract worth

jeopardizing everything those poor people have been

through to finally arrive where they are finally

reaping the fruits of their hardships and labors."

"How can we hold our heads high if we

continually let white folk treat us like we are second

class citizens. If we are truly free, then we should

demand equality and not run from the injustices cast

upon us but seek justice when injustice raises its ugly

head."

"At what expense my wife. This man has the

power to wipe us out. All of us. Everyone may not

agree with your politics. There are some that may

just want to live to a ripe old age and enjoy the fruits of their labors."

Moses was silent. He was thinking.

"Moses, my husband, what is it that you don't understand? This is the same fight we've been fighting all our lives. If we continue to allow the man to threaten and dissuade us when they see fit and for no other reason than that they can then we will never truly be free but just pawns to be used when they see fit.

What we have here is a form of tyranny and it cannot be tolerated. We are building a new America and the day of domination through fear and devastation of Colored folks is over. If we all perish to a man, then that is the way the Good Lord sees it this time but there is a day that things will change, and the veil of racism will one day rise. But everything comes at a price, and I am willing to pay the cost even if it means death.

"And there's no changing my wife even if it means more bloodshed and death? There's no changing your mind my wife?"

Maya shook her head no and Moses saw her eyes well up with tears. Moses took Maya in his arms. He had not bargained for this. He was tired of fighting. All he wanted to do was grow old and sit on the front porch and have a sip or two with Johns and listen to him spin a yarn or two. It wasn't a lot to ask. But Maya had other plans. She was intent on fighting every injustice that came her way. Which meant...

"Then as your husband I stand by your side," Moses said as Maya's cheeks began to drip with the tears of a past that remained present. She didn't want to do this. She did not want any more bloodshed. It was something that she had to do. She'd always fought for the rights of her people and though this might be her toughest battle to date she refused to humble herself for any white man ever again.

Lincoln had emancipated her and as a free person she felt, no, she knew that if she was as free as the next man then with that freedom came equality. No longer would she kow tow to any white man just because. In her eyes those days were long gone. At least in her mind they were and anyone who tried to run roughshod over Maya X was in for a tough time against a very formidable foe.

Moses' words rang in Maya's ears. And stand by her side he did following Maya's winning bid on the dock's contract. Kilpatrick always a man of his word came after New Eden hard.

The first few raids did little to interfere with life at New Eden but if this was just a feeling out period, so Kilpatrick could get a feel for the overall strength of New Eden's defenses we will never know but after being repelled three or four times they changed their tactics.

"Niggras are armed to the teeth. And someone has trained them well too. I'm telling you James my men came back with significant losses on each of our raids. My men say their armed with howitzers and Gatling guns. They say them niggras even got a canon and New Eden is the perfect place to hold off an army if they needed to. They picked the perfect place strategically. There's no cover within five hundred feet of the grounds and that's the only way in. Natural boundaries cover the other three sides to the grounds. They have snipers who are crack shots all along the roads leading up to the front gates. The place is basically impenetrable. I don't know who the brains is behind these niggras but they have some military knowledge."

The tall, robust Mr. Kilpatrick was not used to bad news and chewed on his fat, soggy cigar as he walked around his spacious office before finally resting against the huge, mahogany, desk that sat front and center.

"And as you know we can no longer depend on the Irish. Most of them have gone to work for her now."

"When did this happen? And why wasn't I informed?"

"A few months back. So many had been out of work thanks to M&M that they went up there thinking they were going to run roughshod over a few niggras. They ran into the same thing and after someone killed the leader of that mob she hired anyone who wanted to work and told them to tell their friends. And she's paying more too."

"Those dirty, turncoat, Irish motherfuckers," Kilpatrick said sending the cigar flying out of his mouth. "There's no counting on what these Boston Irish will do next. C'mon Tom. Think. I'm not interested in how proficient they are. I'm more interested in their weaknesses. I'm interested in their downfall, in their total collapse. That's what I'm most interested in."

"Have you ever considered partnering with them James? You could avoid the bloodshed and monopolize the lumber business in the state. I hear tell the woman behind their meteoric rise is as savvy a business woman as you will find."

"I'm not interested in partnering with any one and especially no niggas. To tell you the truth the only thing I'm interested in is eliminating the competition. We've been going about this all wrong. We've got to hit them where it hurts in the pocketbook. I want every load of lumber headed to the docks hit. If they can't meet their contract, then they'll forfeit the bid."

"I'm sorry James. I can't go along with you on this one. We're killing people and for what?

Land. Money. Racism. You have no need for money or land. And you should know that even you will have to answer to the Lord in the end. Think about it James," Thomas said to his oldest friend.

"So, you're not with me on this one. Is that what you're telling me? I can't remember ever going into anything like this without you leading the charge."

"Is that what you want to be known for? It all seems so stupid to me. There are too many alternatives with less hardship and bloodshed. Why can't we all just live in peace?"

"I completely understand Thomas. And I will be expecting you and the missus for our usual Sunday dinner. Do me a favor and send Harold in on your way out."

"Be good James," Thomas said smiling knowing that was not possible.

In the weeks that followed Kilpatrick hit the load on three consecutive days accounting for a total of nine dead including three Irish men escorting the load. Once the Irish found out there was plenty of work and the wages were better they had come in waves and sworn allegiance. All-in-all a fairly good relationship developed between the niggras of New Eden and the Irish. A few had even moved to New Eden to be closer to work. Now three Irish men had been ambushed and killed while at work and without provocation and it was no secret who was behind it.

"And he calls himself an Irishman," one Southie shouted.

There was a loud cry in South Boston that rose as high up as the mayor. But Kilpatrick had been a strong financial backer of the mayor in the last mayoral election. His hands were tied. The Irish well aware of the relationship promptly decided to take matters into their own hands.

"This is not the first time Kilpatrick has done something like this."

"The truth is he doesn't care who he kills as long as he profits. He needs to pay. I was talking to Jamie's widow. She's torn up. You know they just had their first child about a month ago. He won't but twenty-four."

"Damn shame it is. He really should be made to pay."

"They say he's Irish from Dublin."

"He's nothing. He's scum is what he is, and he should be made to pay for his crimes," the man shouted.

"Let's burn him down!" came the cry as the men poured from the pub and into the street intent on seeking retribution in any shape or form.

"Gentlemen, before we go off half-cocked let's come up with some sort of plan," a sober young lad in his early twenties shouted gaining the mobs attention.

"Let's burn him out. He doesn't live far from here," one man shouted out.

"Be sensible man. Everyone knows that he has his own private security guarding his house."

"Yes, and if we start with his businesses he'll be forced to send his security out and that's when we set fire to his home. We don't want the likes of him anywhere near Boston. Let's get rid of him once and for all."

"Okay, so we start with the lumberyard and his stores. I want Casey to take ten or fifteen men and wait 'til we have engaged his security. I'll get word to you and then you can lay waste to his house," the young man said.

"C'mon men. The warehouse and the lumberyard," a man yelled as they headed to their respective locations.

Hours later fires still burned out of control in every section of Boston proper.

James Kilpatrick was livid after going with a large contingent of his own security to assess the damage. The lumberyard resembled a funeral pyre. At no time did James Kilpatrick consider himself the least bit liable for the burning and looting that had taken several of his businesses.

"Mr. Mayor have you seen what these thugs have done," James cried to the mayor.

"I have James. And I'm told this is in reaction to your killing three innocent men."

"I didn't have anything to do with that mayor," Kilpatrick pleaded.

"There's quite a large contingent that believes you did have something to do with it James, so you are being targeted and you only specifically."

"So, you are going to just allow these thugs to burn and loot my businesses?"

"I've done what I can do James. The fire department has a few of them contained but I'm afraid the lumberyard is history. And my fire chief is hesitant about sending his men into harm's way. And those so-called thug are out for blood."

"I want them locked up. Do you hear me? All of them. I want all of them locked up. Ain't nothin' but poor Irish trash getting' all liquored up runnin' 'round burnin' and lootin'. I want a stop put to it immediately," Kilpatrick shouted before heading out and making his way home.

Home he made his way to his study and the bottle of cognac. Pouring himself a little more than four fingers he settled back in his favorite chair and wondered if he hadn't bitten off just a little more than he could handle? But who would have guessed he would have to contend with his own Irishmen. Where was Tom when he needed him. Thomas had foreseen all of this. Why hadn't he listened?

"Mr. Kilpatrick don't you think you and the family would be safer in a hotel in the city?"

"I would feel better if you would stop those thugs from laying waste to my properties," James Kilpatrick yelled.

A small child no more than three or four came running.

"What's wrong daddy?" the little girl said her outstretched arms waiting on her father to pick her up.

"Nothing sweetheart. I was just explaining something to Mr. O'Hara here is all. I guess I got a little excited," Kilpatrick said showing a tender side

seldom seen in him.

"And what about the niggas?"

"They've been quiet so far," O'Hara replied.

Little did they know that all of New Eden was up in arms over this latest strategy.

"Do we just turn our heads and let this go unnoticed?" Maya asked the folks gathered in the newly constructed town hall.

"If we allow this to go unnoticed what's to say that it will not happen again?" Killah asked.

"If we are committed to winning this war with Kilpatrick we have to find a way to send a clear message to him. One that he will think twice about before attempting to inflict any more harm on the residents of New Eden," Johns said.

"Glad to have you on board Johns," Maya said smiling at ol' man Johnson. "I do believe Elise is working on something along those lines. They tell me she rode out of here about an hour ago. And no before you ask. She didn't tell me what she had in mind."

"But I think a clear show of force may be needed about now. I want every man and woman trained to fight to meet here armed to the teeth to meet me right here in a half an hour. Tonight, we ride to Mr. Kilpatrick's home and give him a ten-gun salute."

There was wild cheering when this announcement was made. And in minutes most of the folks were mounted up and ready to go.

Maya and Moses led the way at steady gait on the new Arabian horses Maya had seen fit to cross breed with some wild mustangs she'd acquired from somewhere. The crossbreed proved a pretty large horse with an agileness and fleet of hoof not found in the local breeds.

Many of the troops had also purchased the crossbreeds from Maya and the army stood tall and proud in the saddle. Arriving an hour later at the gates of the Kilpatrick estate. Killah easily apprehended the sentry while Moses quickly disposed of the other one. Now on the spacious grounds in front of the main house. Moses had his troops spread out. It was just about this time that James Kilpatrick was persuaded by both O'Hara and his wife that he would be safer within Boston city limits. The minute James Kilpatrick opened the front door baby girl in his arms he realized how right O'Hara and his wife were.

As far as he could see there was a sea of brown faces of all different hues. Putting his daughter down James Kilpatrick considered going for his gun then considered how foolish that would have been. Unfortunately, O'Hara's thought process was not that sophisticated, and he was quickly shot down before he could clear his holster. The child screamed seeing this and Maya quickly walked over to the child wrapping her brown arms around her with the hopes of comforting the small child. The girl calmed down quickly under Maya's watch.

"Where are you niggas going with my daughter?" Kilpatrick screamed the tears flowing down his face.

"Don't worry. As long as we are allowed to operate unimpeded your daughter will be safe with us but anymore attacks on innocent people and I'll dismember her limb from tiny limb. Do you understand? Ask around about me. My name is Maya X," she said before turning and riding away with the child in her arms.

"Bye mommy. Bye daddy," the little girl yelled back at her parents.

"What have you done now James? What have you done that they took our daughter. What have you done James?" his wife yelled as she swung repeatedly at her husband..

James Kilpatrick took his sobbing wife into his arms and did his best to console her.

Elise appeared form the wooded forest.

"You beat me to it. Although I would have personally taken both wife and child," Elise said grinning broadly.

"Then you weren't being very observant my daughter. That man could care less about her. She has served her function. She has given him a child. But she has no purpose. Now this little girl means all the world to him and as long as we have her we will have peace."

"You must know you can't keep her."

"I dare him to go to the authorities. He's not going to do anything that he thinks will jeopardize his little girl's life."

"How long do you plan on keeping her?"

"Twenty maybe thirty years," Maya said as she and Elise broke into a good laugh.

"Hello wife," Moses said riding up alongside the two women now.

"Hello yourself," Maya replied. "Is this the same husband who did everything short of begging me not go head up against Kilpatrick because I had no chance of beating such a wealthy and powerful man."

"Don't gloat. This is not over yet. Not by any means."

"And as long as I have the Good Lord on my side I never worry about it being over or being defeated. How can I lose with you and the Good Lord on your side?" Maya smiled.

An hour and a half later they were met at the gate by a perimeter that made Maya proud. All was untouched, and Maya had Moses switch the guard out and double it. Every man was paid for their guard duty and many welcomed it as a night to get away from their wives and spend a night with the boys even if guard duty required complete silence.

Elise volunteered to take the little girl and care for her in the time she was at New Eden and Maya put her mind to parlaying the child into a truce with Kilpatrick.

Two days later after countless couriers came bringing notes from Kilpatrick begging for the return of his daughter at any cost. He even said that he would relinquish his pursuit of the docks.

Maya was content to let him plead his case refusing to acknowledge any of his correspondence. When all else failed he sent his emissary and oldest friend Thomas to see if he could talk any sense to this uppity nigga.

"Miss Maya, I presume. Moses? It is quite humbling to meet you two. I've been following your

rise to the top of the Boston business world. It has
been a meteoric rise to say the least. I am only sorry
that we had to meet under these circumstances. I will
tell you that I resigned from my position with Mr.
Kilpatrick when he told me of his plans to bring
M&M Lumber to its knees. But that is not why I
resigned. I did not want to see any unneeded
bloodshed. He proceeded without me and this is what
it has resulted in. His wife is on the verge of a
nervous breakdown and he is quite distraught as well
and would like to know what it will take for him to
get his daughter back."

"Mr. Greeley is it?"

"Yes, but you can call me Tom." The man
smiled.

"Mr. Greeley you better than anyone else
knows Mr. Kilpatrick's assets. What would it take to
break him? And would he give it all up for his
daughter?"

"That's a tough question. If I were to gather an educated guess I would say he's worth somewhere in the neighborhood of a couple of million."

"Then this is what I suggest. I want the ownership of all land deeds and businesses Kilpatrick owns. I will allow him to continue his current lifestyle, but I want ownership of all land and businesses. Is that understood?"

"It is, and I will relay the message to him promptly. And again, it is my honor to meet you both."

Neither Maya nor Moses responded and when he held out his hand to Moses Moses did not return the gesture and simply opened the front door for the man to leave. When he was gone Maya turned to Moses.

"Do you think he was sincere?"

"I do," Moses replied.

"Then why didn't you shake his hand?"

"Because we are at war and I will not pretend to be friendly with the man who threatens me or mine with harm."

"How do you think my offer will play out?"

"Depends on how much he loves his daughter."

They didn't have to wait long. James Kilpatrick responded the following day conceding to every concession Maya had drawn up including leaving the state and turning over all worldly assets to the owners of M&M Lumber.

Maya and Moses were now the largest landowners and lumber business in the state. And with Elise now covering the books on the daily there was little left for Moses and Maya to do but guard the front porch from unwanted visitors. And being that Boston was quite a distance after a few drinks Moses and Johns opened a little upscale tavern which

brought folks for miles around. Now the two friends

saw each other on a daily basis, well that was when

Maya and little Paul allowed Moses to leave the front

porch.